WILLIAM BELL

WILLIAM BELL

Copyright © 2019 Betsy Hayhow Hemming

Typesetting and Cover Design by FormattingExperts.com

ISBN 978-0-578-56708-2

To my Mom, who was William's biggest supporter

BETSY HAYHOW HEMMING

WILLIAM
BELL

INTRODUCTION

Dearest Reader:

Allow me to introduce myself. My name is William Bell. I could give you an ordinary introduction, including my age, my occupation, and my background, even my skin color. But my life isn't that ordinary, and frankly, that type of information is meaningless in the scheme of things.

However, I have inserted myself at the beginning of this book to urge you to keep an open mind. You will be reading all sorts of interesting descriptions of me and I want to get my two cents in first. Unequivocally, everything you will read about me is absolutely true. Now, I must quickly amend such a strong statement with the observation that truth is in the eyes of the beholder. You are about to meet a few of these beholders of truth. Their tales are interesting and involve passion of one sort or another. They certainly have decided views of me, all of which will emerge as they tell their stories.

Specifically, you will meet three individuals, just normal human beings trying to make their way in life. Debra dreams of houses and suffers a tragedy in her life. Sam loses his job but gains new insights into his reason for being. And Emma, a fairly intense attorney, imagines owning a horse farm. That sounds simple but, of course, there's much more to it.

Just normal human beings, as mentioned.

What is my connection with these people? Consider me a facilitator, if you will – a facilitator of life. It's a rather absurd description, but it's the best I have been able to articulate. I am sure that you have many questions on just what a life facilitator does, and I hope you will gain your answers in the stories to come.

—William Bell

DEBRA

William here:

I'd like to introduce you to Debra. I must chuckle for a moment, pardon me. For I didn't discover Debra; she discovered me – in her dreams. I can imagine your face and you think I'm pushing the envelope a tad now, don't you? I will be my most factual. She actually discovered my office in her dreams. Then, she found the office in the light of day and was compelled to visit, and in doing so, met me. She was quite hesitant to share her story with the stranger who lived in a house of her dreams. Not the *house of her dreams – simply one of many.*

For Debra dreams of houses. Some are recurring dreams, therefore, recurring houses. Some are new to her. Some are furnished; some are empty, awaiting an owner. Some are scary; some are chock full of junk; some are labyrinths that go on forever. I must admit that I am absolutely fascinated by Debra and her dreams. The question is, whatever do they mean and how can I be of assistance to someone who is struggling with a major life issue and doesn't even know it – or know me for that matter?

– William

1

I've not been here before. The house is cold and empty, and it's entirely made of stone. I walk alone into a great room, icy and still. I peer through the shadows at the giant stone fireplace, its grate clean, but dusty from disuse. The space looks so empty and abandoned. One could imagine a fine roaring fire, a dark red Persian carpet in front of the hearth, even a mammoth dog sleeping peacefully, but waiting to pounce on the unsuspecting stranger.

I cross the glacial room, go through the doorway and enter a long hall. Nails and hooks mar the smooth slabs of the stone walls, where mighty framed pictures once hung proudly. I must go down that hallway. At the end, I come to a closed door, a heavy wooden one with no window. I don't even pause to ponder what's on the other side. Opening the door, I enter a smaller room, cozier, if any stone room can be that. It's empty as well, and this time, I can imagine a study, with candles lit, a paper-strewn desk, a cat on the window seat. On it goes. Stone room after stone room after stone room. More doors to open, more hallways to traverse. No one is here; it's silent, so very silent. So cold …

I awoke to the radio playing soft jazz, as I do every morning, and stretched in the warmth of the bed. I grabbed my dream journal and began to write down as much detail of the house as I could. This was a new house, one I hadn't visited before. I eagerly jotted down my tour through the cold stone house, writing rapidly before my hazy memories began to fade as my brain acknowledged the new morning.

I chuckled to myself as I journaled. "My name is Debra Kelly and I am a house-dreamer," I would say at Dreamers Anonymous if there was such a thing. I flicked through the pages of the journal, chock-full of dreams about houses. Of course, I do dream about other things as well, but the house dreams outweigh all other content by about 50 to 1. I shut the book and jumped out of bed. It was another gorgeous morning in Michigan, and it was time to get going. Daniel – my husband – had zipped out of the house hours ago.

Beyond my surreal, poorly-paying career as a house dreamer, I work as a social worker at a local hospital. Daniel and I live in a contemporary bungalow in Royal Oak, one of the artsy burbs of metro Detroit. The bungalow has a special energy and I was drawn to it instantly. As our realtor said, "the house has potential."

It's no wonder I dream of houses and, I am pleased to say, some components of my dreams have made their way into the slow but sure renovation of our home. Now, it welcomes me in each night, its warm autumn-colored rooms filled with great finds from local consignment shops.

I chose social work for several reasons. First, I came into life a little bit earlier than the average baby, meaning that my first dwelling was an incubator at the very hospital where I now work. Fortunately, my hospital stay was short-lived, given a life-long stubbornness that apparently cranked up immediately upon being placed in said incubator. "Get me out of here!" I think I must have said in loud baby-cry. While I got out of the hospital in record speed, I did grow up to be a tad more petite than the average gal and the stubbornness grew at a more rapid pace than my arms and legs. It's served me well over the years; I use it in my work every day. Another life-long trait is not so easy to explain. The politically-correct explanation is that I tend to be innovative and unique in my thinking.

The truth of it is that I've "sensed" things all of my life, and I awkwardly learned in high school that others don't necessarily "sense" the same things. It is not hip to comment on what another person – particularly the opposite sex – is thinking when they have not voiced the words. A phrase such as "I like you, too" takes on dark meaning in that case, and I, unfortunately, acquired somewhat of a reputation for being weird. While I learned to manage this special little quirk, I was curious as to whether others had a similar gift. When I would run into someone I liked, I would think "can you hear me?" to see if there was any reaction. There never was, though I do remember one boy blushing and moving quickly down the hall. I can't be sure if it was teen-age angst or something deeper. I keep it pretty buttoned up these days but hoped it would be an asset at work.

I am married to the previously-mentioned Daniel, who is a manufacturer's rep for the auto industry. That means he promotes cars and the parts cars are made of. No, he didn't hear me either when we met, but I was okay with that. He reeked of normal and I yearned for that quality at that point in my life.

We met as normal people do: We crashed into each other at the door of a coffee shop in the hospital lobby. Unlike the movies, where coffee spills daintily on the floor and the soon-to-be-couple gaze into each other's eyes, our crash was a real disaster. I ended up screeching for ice for the burns on my hands, while Daniel sat on the floor, dazed, not by my beauty, but by the fall he took from slipping on said coffee.

But instead of both fleeing the scene in revulsion, we started to laugh. Daniel was the knight in shining armor who got back on his feet and was sharp enough to get not only a laugh but a phone number from me. One thing led to another and we married six months later.

As mentioned, I was intrigued by his normalcy and we quickly entered into a very conventional married life. I won't use the word "boring," but … Daniel is a creature of habit. He follows a strict work schedule and a strict diet. He also isn't around a great deal, as he spends most of his life in his car, representing some of the small auto suppliers in town and across the country.

His travel really doesn't bother me. I can entertain myself quite nicely, and normal Daniel seemed the right decision at the time. Besides, any man who will voluntarily and lovingly wash his wife's hair is a darn good find indeed. Yep. He does. Every once in a while, if our paths cross in the bathroom and I'm doing a quick wash of my hair in the sink, he will take over and gently scrub my scalp and then thoroughly rinse my hair. It is a joy, for sure. He even rubs my feet at night. He may be Mr. Boring but he's *my* Mr. Boring.

We also have two felines right out of the play "Cats." Mr. Mistoffelees and Grizabella have been faithful friends for many years. It's always comforting to be able to rationalize noises in the night, especially when Daniel is gone. "Why it's only those crazy cats," I've said many a dark evening when some crash or odd noise pulled me away from some fascinating dream house.

They are mellow kitties, quite content to settle in the window as I depart for the hospital each morning. "Mellow," like the word "normal," is good, because that's not how I would describe my work environment. Hospital social workers have an interesting role in the medical world. We weave in and out of people's lives, usually during times of great crisis. We also must weave in and out of the working world of the medical personnel, some of whom respect our role and many who simply don't.

The pay is so-so, the stress is high, and the intrinsic reward of a job well done is fairly non-existent – except for the occasional miracles. I was drawn to the career because it seemed a good place to utilize my intuition, but it hasn't seemed to work out that way. I long to find something more fulfilling, but I can't put my arms around exactly what that something should be. I wonder if my restlessness is connected to my incessant dreaming, not that it's a bad thing. Time will tell, I'm sure.

2

The expressionless man sits in a dirty white plastic chair in his yard, in front of his off-white brick ranch. He almost blends in with the house, with his white short-sleeved shirt and loose white pants. He pays no attention as I walk in his front door and make a right turn into a bedroom. It is cozy, as bedrooms go, with two twin beds covered in bright red and blue wool blankets. I am curious about the man outside, but I continue on, walking into the next room, another bedroom. This one is filled with beds, all shapes and sizes, arranged in different sections of the room like sub-bedrooms. A large king bed with wooden headboard and matching dresser take up one side of the room. A trundle bed, with lacy bedspread, and rocking chair occupy another area. A little ramp leads the way to a third space, this one with four bunk beds. I can see beyond the beds to more rooms, all filled with beds. But the alarm by one of the beds started to go off and simply won't stop …

Hmmmm … It was my alarm that was going off and the bedrooms vanished into thin air. I awoke, a bit on the grumpy side, as recognition dawned – much like the morning was doing outside – that it was only Wednesday, and I needed to get up and head to the hospital.

I quickly jotted down what I could recall from my dream, thinking about the odd man dressed in white, then reluctantly departed the coziness of my bed on this early spring morning. Any nighttime warmth from my personal furnace named Daniel was long gone; not even the smell of shaving lotion lingered in the bathroom. I shook my head and smiled

12

a half smile; it was almost like living with a ghost. His travel would keep him away for a couple of nights, but we would have a lovely dinner out on Friday night.

A pat on the head to the kitties, and I was off, facing another day of medical angst and malaise. I kept thinking about beds but wasn't sure if it was my attempt to analyze my morning's dream or a desperate desire to return to the safe haven of my night-time nest.

The morning passed slowly, and I was glad to join my best friend Cate for lunch. We grew up together, and it's amazing to me that we remain connected. She and I have extremely different personalities, but once we figured out how to leverage that, we've become and remained the best of friends, both working in the medical profession. She is the one person who I can tell about my dreams. Nope, I don't share them with my husband. I tried once, early in our relationship, and Daniel appeared horrified. He stated unequivocally that he doesn't dream. I, of course, asked how it could be possible not to dream, but Daniel got a look in his eye suggesting that this wasn't a normal topic of conversation for him and we moved on to other things.

Cate is the perfect candidate to lend a listening ear because she is a helicopter pilot – one of those caring individuals who go to strange places in the dead of night to pick up human organs and bring them back to the hospital for transplant. Her perspective on life is different, plain and simple. I don't sense she dreams much at night, but she's always been willing to provide comment on my copious journeys into dreamland.

Today was no different. "What's with all the beds?" she asked, after I shared my latest creative nighttime venture.

"I don't know!" I said, rolling my eyes. This dream thing has been such a constant in my life that I have ups and downs in dealing with it. Some years, I analyze the heck out of my dreams, actively seeking answers; in other years, I let them flow on without seeking any insight from them.

"Let's see: the number of children I will have someday? Maybe the number of husbands? Oh, wait: The number of asshole bosses I have to endure."

We laughed and enjoyed our lunches – mine a soup and a salad, Cate's a fat burger and fries. Helicopter pilots must really burn the calories, I thought, looking at my tall twig of a friend.

Cate took a big bite of burger and turned her warm brown eyes to me. "Seriously," she said while attempting to swallow the bite, "I know you've had all these dreams like forever, but it seems like you are a little unsettled or something about it today. What's up?"

I picked at my salad, thinking about how well she knew me. "I don't know," I said once again, this time in a monotone. "I'm sort of itchy and agitated. I don't know if it's the dreams, or the job, or both. But something has to change."

She nodded. Cate was well aware of the intensity of my job, not to mention the steady state of my marriage. She has repeatedly shaken her head when I've talked about Daniel and how comfortable my relationship is with him, believing that I lacked key elements of a successful relationship, such as passion, emotion and intensity, to quote a few. It was no surprise to sense her shift to one of her favorite topics. "Have you thought it might be your marriage?" she asked in a not-very-delicate way. "And who is the dude in the dream, by the way?"

"Let's not go there today, okay?" I retorted, suddenly frustrated by the conversation.

Cate shook her head yet again. "That's right; shut it all in like always," she said, taking another huge bite of her burger. I returned to picking at my salad.

14

3

"We'll never get this place clean," I muttered.

"Then work harder!" snapped an angry man I had never seen before.

I looked up, sweaty and grimy. The basement smelled so moldy and awful that I thought about unplugging my nose in order to better yell at him. Nope. It wasn't worth the effort, and I went back to the endless job of picking up damp, mildewed clothing and stuffing it into an endless series of black garbage bags. He marched up the stairs, leaving me alone in the clammy, chilly room. I looked around to gauge how much more work I had to do. The job was never-ending; the room was filled with crap – clothes, toys, broken furniture, musty books, boxes filled with who knows what, falling apart from the moisture. I walked into the next room, and gasped. This room was filled floor to ceiling with shelves overflowing with stuff. And I had to deal with it all.

I awoke with a snort – I could still smell the mold and mildew from my dream. After a few moments, I did manage to persuade myself that it was just a dream. Too weary to put that classic on paper, I slowly crept out of bed and got ready for another day. Even the cats could sense I was lacking my normal energetic step; they followed me throughout the house as I went through the motions of my morning.

It was a barn-burner of a day at the hospital, climaxing in an all-out war with a doctor and my supervisor over the lack of emotional support of a very ill patient. Sadly, this happens on a regular basis with this doctor. I seethed all the way home. Idiots – they are all idiots, I concluded fiercely. One of my core job components is patient satisfaction. If a doctor consistently makes patients cry, we have a problem. It didn't seem like rocket science to me. Sadly, the doctor doesn't see it that way, and complains to my supervisor – who stands up for the doctor. So what if the doctor brings in a gazillion dollars each year for the hospital in research grants. I idealistically thought the hospital's primary purpose is to heal the patient. The situation is not made easier by the fact that my intuition has served me very well in truly understanding patient situations. I sense he becomes enraged when I can report so much detail about his poor behavior.

The cats chattered nervously when I arrived home. My mood was not any better than when I had left that morning and I gained no pleasure from my Daniel-gone routine of dinner eaten while reading a bad novel, cuddled in one of the coziest couches on the planet in our living room. I must confess that it is pretty pleasant to eat dinner with one's nose in a book, a treat I only give myself when Daniel is traveling. My favorite novels are those romantic mystery thrillers where a strong woman inherits a crumbling old mansion. I get the irony. But this was one night when the book failed to deliver, and I finally had to say "uncle" and call it an early night. Daniel would be home at some god-awful time, around the midnight hour or later, which would cause sleepus interruptus, so it probably made sense to start the process of heading to bed.

But I found I was not looking forward to the dreams this night, which is quite odd for me. I sighed heavily a few times and finally slipped into dreamland without knowing it.

4

He comes up behind me, as he does every so often, grabs the water cup, fills it with warm water, and pours it down my soapy head over the sink. I purr contentedly. He fills a second glass, then a third. He tenderly takes up the mass of wet locks and squeezes the excess water out into the sink. Then, he caresses my shoulders and says, "There, babe. It's all done."

I look up in the mirror to give him a special smile of thanks, as I always do. But no one is there. I whip my wet head around, glancing in every corner of the room. It is empty.

I emerged from the dream with a horrific start, very early in the morning, as the first crack of dawn slithered into the room. This dream wasn't about houses. I had been in my own bathroom, with Daniel. He had been washing my hair. He used to do that all the time, many moons ago. But he hadn't been around much as of late. I quickly realized that Daniel was not home yet. I also knew deep within my soul that something very bad had happened to Daniel.

It wasn't a surprise when the phone rang a short hour later, after I'd struggled to shower and dress in what I hoped was appropriate clothing for the expected call to come and dried the culpable locks of hair. I did try to keep my brain from coming to conclusions, with little success. I called his cell phone, repeatedly. There was no answer and frankly, I didn't expect one.

Though I knew the phone would ring, I still jumped.

"Is this Debra Kelly?"

"Yes," I said, trying to tame the jitters. What I wanted to

say: "I know why you are calling. I KNOW ALREADY!" But I didn't take liberties.

"This is Officer Davidson from the State Police. Mrs. Kelly, I would like to confirm that Daniel Kelly is your husband?"

"Yes," I said, my voice cracking ever so slightly.

"Mrs. Kelly, your husband has been in an accident."

Later, I would think back to this moment and feel like I had been an unwilling participant in a really bad play. But in the moment, I found that I wanted to calmly and clearly communicate to the nice officer: "I know that something really awful has happened to my husband, so please get to the point." But, of course, that wouldn't be appropriate. I didn't know what to say.

"Excuse me?" I said, trying to buy a second of time.

"We need you to come to the hospital," the soft-gruff voice said. "Can you drive yourself there?"

I sat still, disconnected phone in hand, pets at my side. Did the cats know something, sense something? I checked in with myself, realizing for the first time that I wasn't screaming. I wasn't crying. I wasn't kicking a chair. I rationalized my lack of emotion as shock, as I carefully put the phone away and moved to the bathroom of my very recent dream – nightmare might be a better word at this point – to finish getting ready.

They were calm and comforting at the hospital, the EMTs explaining the horrible car accident on I-94 in the middle of the night, that he was dead at the scene, the car totaled. The other driver, an elderly woman, simply slid over the median into the oncoming traffic, right into his car. She died as well, perhaps of a heart attack; they didn't know yet. What a tragedy … our sympathies … Are you the next of kin? Do you have a funeral home in mind?

So began the blur of the next many days, with calls to stricken family members, attempts to comfort Daniel's grieving parents, the funeral plans and never-ending red tape caused by a horrific incomprehensible death. I had no answers to some burning questions: Why was an elderly woman driving so late at night? Why was Daniel so late in coming home? Why wasn't I a sobbing mess?

5

Daniel and I are enjoying dinner at a restaurant. Perhaps it's our anniversary; he smiles at me and raises his wine glass for a toast. I grin, happy that we are together, and that he is back from his trip. The waiter brings our food and we begin to eat, as we gaze at one another. I feel so close to him right now. A man in a blue uniform appears at the table. I look up at him, questioningly. It appears he is a police officer. "Ma'am, I'm sorry to inform you that your husband has died in a car accident," the man states in a serious tone. I laugh at him. "Silly you, my husband is right here," I reply. I turn back to Daniel and the chair is empty. I scream and sob for Daniel and the officer says, "I'm sorry," over and over and over again …

I awoke, already dreading the day. After such a painful dream, I wondered if I would feel his presence in the house. But I didn't, confirming that he had truly gone away that day in the bathroom – and wouldn't be back. Even with that realization, I still couldn't find a single tear to shed, unlike the Debra in my dream.

The funeral was very lovely as funerals go. I've been to my fair share, though never so personally. I barely remember the drive but, there I was, sitting in the front row at the funeral home, with Daniel's sobbing parents on each side of me. His sister, bent over with head in hands, was down the row with her stoic husband and two teen-aged children, who both looked crushed. The room was filled with family, friends, Daniel's colleagues, my colleagues.

I know there's supposed to be something comforting about the rituals of a funeral, but I stood at the back of the room with numb heart and tearless eyes following the brief service, as person after person came up to share their warm memories of Daniel. At the cemetery, I literally held up my mother-in-law as she placed a rose on top of the coffin. I then offered my own contribution – a carnation – and wondered about our flower choices.

What is wrong with me?

But I knew.

I took a few days off work as people who have lost a spouse should do. I knew that it was time to address this lack of grieving widow stuff, but it was not to be. I remained clear-eyed and free of dreams while my brain focused on the morning of Daniel's death. That precluded any mourning of his loss, as did my efforts to keep busy by eradicating Daniel's presence from the house.

Because of my history as a bizarre little girl who tried to talk to people through her mind, I knew that my dream of Daniel in the bathroom wasn't out of the scope of some of my past experiences. In high school, beyond trying to mentally connect with guys, I realized that I knew things that others did not fathom. I guess one would call them premonitions. I would have strange feelings about a friend, and the friend's mom would die. I would get upset in a class and learn that some of the kids had cheated on a test. I never had all the facts, just incredibly strong feelings, which always meant something.

I was okay with that. I knew that my ambitions to help others deal with the fascinating world of "normal" connected directly to my interesting way of being. I even figured I could use my vast experience with abnormality to benefit the world.

21

I was admitted to the social work program at Wayne State University in Detroit and, much to my surprise, discovered that there were a whole lot of abnormalities out there including many of my fellow students right in the classroom, not to mention those at the hospital – and I am not talking about the patients.

That's why it was such a delight to have dear Daniel in my life. From the moment I crashed into him, he kept things in a state of peace through his steady approach to life. Five years later, when we should have been celebrating a milestone anniversary in a few short weeks, he was dead, and I was a widow. What a strange word, "widow." It sounds so dark, so ugly, so alone. I shuddered as the image of a black widow spider sprang into my mind. On that note, I decided that "widow" was a word to be stricken from my vocabulary. My brain also quickly returned to the little scene in the bathroom on the morning of Daniel's death, and I vowed never to wash my hair in the sink again. I shook my head, not for the first time, at the reality of that quasi-dream.

As I packed boxes of Daniel's practical clothing – tan slacks, dark blazers, pristine loafers, pressed jeans – I chewed on whether my recent apathy was connected to this very normal life of mine. I also struggled to understand my dream and whether it heralded a return to my premonitions of the past. What would happen now that I was on my own again? I leaned against a now-packed box and realized that I didn't really want to go to sleep that night.

6

Daniel kisses me goodbye and jumps into a fancy red convertible. He opens the window and waves his hand as he speeds down the short driveway. I wave back, saddened that Daniel must leave again so soon, then shake my head and start to turn to walk back into the house. Suddenly, the brake lights on the car come on and it screeches to a halt. Daniel jumps out but he's not Daniel! He is a tall, slender man who I don't know at all. "Daniel is gone," he says to me, then gets back into the car and turns into the street. I run down the driveway, yelling "WAIT!" But it's too late. The car disappears around the corner.

I woke up sweaty and grumpy. I remembered avoiding the concept of sleep last night, and I had been right. What a weird dream, I thought, as I contemplated another day with barely enough energy to move my pinkie finger. Forget capturing this dream in my journal; it would only exhaust me further.

Wearily, I forced myself out of bed, knowing that today was my last day on leave from my job. I had a long list of things to do, including the minor tasks of cleaning out the past and getting ready for a new reality. At least that was my plan. But that fabricated list didn't come close to getting at the essence of the issue – my fabricated grief regarding Daniel's death. Tomorrow, I would go back to doing battle with the bad-mannered doctor, who I had dubbed Dr. Evil, and my completely unsupportive boss. Worse, I would have to face my colleagues and act out a set of emotions I simply did not feel. I am not sure why. There, I confessed the crux of the dilemma to myself and no amount of packing up clothes would resolve it, I knew. But attempting to tackle the list was as good as it was going to get.

The phone interrupted my reflections. "Cate," I said aloud, knowing it was her. I let the phone ring, understanding that her noble intentions were to get me out of the house and breathing fresh air. Not today. I would spend the day as planned and see if I could craft enough mental armor to make it through tomorrow.

7

The Victorian house is warmly lit as I walk by. A handsome three-story home on the corner, it clearly has been well cared for over the years. Painted the right hue of off-white with pine green shutters and a red door, the house looks proud of itself in the dark of night. I pause, drinking in the splendor of the place. This house is well-loved, I can tell. It is so welcoming that I walk right up to the large front porch, climb the steps that are home to the expected red geraniums, and open the front door.

The fresh smell of lavender envelopes me. A slight breeze floats through from a ceiling fan, high up in the foyer. The walls are painted a soothing sage green and small lights mounted on the walls warm the space. A set of wind chimes tinkle gently from somewhere nearby.

NO, NO, NO! I don't want to wake up; this is a NICE dream! The cats scattered as I whipped off the comforter, stalked over to my alarm clock and smacked it until it quieted. Note to self: An alarm clock that sounds like wind chimes might be an excellent future purchase.

I thought fondly of the house in my dream and returned to bed to jot down a few notes in my journal. What a contrast to the prior night. This house felt so comfortable and familiar, so calming and peaceful.

Reality soon emerged. An ache settled in the pit of my stomach as I began getting ready for the day ahead. I pondered the closet, now devoted solely to my clothing, as I had managed to remove all vestiges of Daniel's existence in the sizeable walk-in space. Why did I have to clear all traces of Daniel so quickly? I shook my head and moved on to other dilemmas: What does one wear when one returns to her job as a new widow? Black? Too obvious. Black and white? Too intentional. Red? Don't go there. I settled on a blue top and tan slacks after investing way too much time, and rushed to force down something of a breakfast, feed the cats and get out of the door.

I was late to work, which was no surprise; I figured I would get a free pass from the powers that be. But even with the extensive reflections from the previous day, I wasn't prepared for the outpouring of condolences and support the minute I stepped into the administrative offices at the hospital.

"Debra, dear," cooed my boss, coming in for the full hug. Carol Phillips was a solid woman, not in a good sense, and I shrunk in trepidation. "I am so very sorry, my dear."

I sensed her complete insincerity, knowing that it was all for show. Ironically, the others awaiting their turn clucked their appreciation at her concern. I knew better but forced what I hoped would be viewed as a tentative smile from a grieving widow. "Thank you uh, thanks to all of you; the fruit basket was so lovely. If you don't mind, I'll go have a quiet moment before I get started."

I took off down the hallway of gray cubicle space with a fake little smile. Can one have a quiet moment in a cubicle? I was going to try, though my radar was on full alert, and sure enough, the line of concerned co-workers began forming immediately.

So went the morning. Lunch consisted of leftovers from the funeral, from the substantive stash of small plastic containers in my freezer. As I attempted digestion, the phone rang. As usual, I identified the caller before picking up the receiver, forcing the food to stay put in my stomach. Perhaps I was feeling more pain that I realized.

"Yes Carol?" I said.

My boss paused for a moment, then started speaking quickly. "I know you are just back from your leave, but I need you to come to my office right now. Dr. McCrory is here as well."

Great. Dr. Evil and my boss. I knew that my advocating on behalf of his latest frustrated patient would come back to bite me and it appeared the time of reckoning had arrived. Why did it have to be so hard to help people get a little respect while recuperating at the hospital? As I walked down the hall, it struck me that I had significantly more emotion about my spat with the doctor than the death of my husband.

8

Doors. So many doors. I continue walking down the narrow aisle; it's rather dark and very dusty. The queue of doors of all sizes and colors continues, some old and battered, some looking like emerging art. It's quiet; a lone rotary fan struggles to offer a snippet of air. I could make door art, I think. Suddenly, a dull red door falls on its side right in front of me. I jump, of course. How random! Then another door falls, and another. The window glass in one explodes across the floor. I start backing up the aisle and the doors follow me ...

Bleary-eyed, I get out of bed, shaking my head. I am the queen of weird dreams, but this one was a little scary. It was only about doors, but there was something dreadful about them. I couldn't put my finger on it.

Usually Fridays put a bounce in my step, as I think about the possibility called the weekend. But work remained an emotional drain and facing a weekend without relief sounded dismal at best. I was exhausted. The meeting with Carol and Dr. McCrory had been awful beyond measure. "Dear Debra," Dr. McCrory had crooned. "So very sorry about your loss." His tone instantly became terse. "But we simply must clarify our roles and my expectations. I am the doctor, not you." After about five more minutes of his outrage and rebuke, with Carol nodding very seriously at every accusation, I sent a strong mental note of indignation to the dear doctor. I sure hoped the patient would let the hospital have it when filling out the satisfaction survey. I knew I hadn't heard the end of this disaster.

Even worse was the mental effort of appearing mournful every day, which was taking its toll. It wasn't that I was all chirpy and fun-loving, but deep in my heart, I knew that the stronger emotion was confusion, rather than grief. Finally back at home, I dragged myself into the kitchen and watched the cats scurry away, then creep back for their meal. Their motivation was to avoid me, yet still be fed, I figured. I didn't blame them; I wanted to avoid me too.

That evening followed a new nightly pattern of force-feeding myself, a futile attempt to keep busy by cleaning or organizing, then a glass of wine to hopefully allow a few moments of peace before summoning up the courage to go to bed. For the first time ever, I began to dread the night with its increasingly eerie dreams.

9

There. Doesn't that look nice? A beautiful red door, freshly paint-
ed and installed. I take a step back and admire my handiwork.
A yellow butterfly circles the porch and I smile. It begins an explo-
ration of this fine new door. But wait! It gets too close. Its wings
flutter and stick to the fresh paint. It can't get free. I desperately
try to brush it away before its delicate wings are damaged, but
I am too late. It frantically beats against the door and I finally
flick it to the ground, knowing that its life is over. I find myself
tearing up. I look up at the door and see the stain left by the
butterfly's wings. The door is ruined; I killed the butterfly ...

My loud whimpering woke me up early. What an awful
dream. The desperate fluttering of the butterfly remained
seared in my brain. I sat up and looked around, then plopped
back down and covered my head with the comforter. This day
was over, as far as I was concerned. The cats were nowhere
to be seen.

10

I drive endlessly in the dusk of the evening, passing rows of houses. It's odd how so many different and unique homes can co-exist in the same neighborhood! I am bewildered by the extremes. The one to the right goes on forever; how could one house have so many wings? Oh, the one down the street is one I've seen before! It's that beautiful mansion. I can even hear the wind chimes, their tones growing distant as I drive past. I think I see a shadow of a man on the porch, but I am past the house and can't see clearly. Now the houses grow more ominous. They come closer and closer, looming over me; it's sickly cold. I press harder on the accelerator, to escape. The houses start to moan – wait, that doesn't make sense. I must get out of here, must get out of here, must get out of here …

I practiced denial as I arose from bed and headed to the bathroom, refusing to think about the dream that had left me sweaty and cold all at the same time. Suddenly, I sank to the floor and began to weep. What happened to me in the three weeks since Daniel's death? I had the urgent need to vomit.

It took all my strength to rise from the chilly bathroom floor and get ready for work. I refused to call in sick; I would not succumb to this despair, seemingly comprised of a strange conundrum of guilt, imagination and depression. Is this what constitutes grieving? My psych classes sure described grief differently. I shook my head as I wrapped a scarf around my neck, a weak attempt at comfort, and headed to another nightmare called work.

Needless to say, the day did not go well. I could barely communicate, let alone demonstrate empathy with angry family members of ill patients. I finally gave up the ghost in the late afternoon; with no meetings on the calendar, I slid out of work a bit early.

As I drove into the driveway, my cell phone began to buzz. I parked in the garage and greeted Cate: "Hey there!" I said, in an artificially bright voice, hoping valiantly that she would be too geeked about something, anything, to notice.

"Hey! I know this is last-minute, but I got a certificate for dinner for two at Hadley's in Birmingham. Do you want to come?"

I instantly analyzed the options of hiding at home or enduring the high energy of my dear friend. Amazingly, I found myself agreeing to dinner. "Okay," I replied. "But what is Hadley's? I've never heard of it before."

"I hadn't either," she said. "It's a new restaurant, on the southern edge of town, and we got gift certificates as a thank-you for one of our trips. I immediately thought of you."

I smiled wanly to myself. I knew she worried about me, having not seen me since the funeral, and I knew that she probably had worked hard to figure out a way to get me out of the house. "It's a deal," I said. "Where should I meet you?"

"I checked, and there's a small parking structure on Peabody Street. Park, and I'll meet you there. We'll walk around the corner to Hadley's. It's supposed to be very quaint."

We agreed on timing and I walked into the house. The cats seemed to do a quick assessment of my mood, concluded that it was improved, and put on a little kitty show, probably to demonstrate that they were worthy of a nice tuna dinner. I rewarded their effort, then changed into a pair of dark jeans and a teal-colored sweater before jumping into the car and heading to Birmingham. I knew where the parking structure was, if not the restaurant, and found Cate waiting for me by the entrance to the deck. I waved and parked my car, then jumped out to meet her.

"It's around the block," Cate said as she started walking down the street. But I was not at her side. Nope. I was statue-still, staring dumbfoundedly at the house across the street. A big Victorian house. Three stories. Pine-green shutters. A red front door. I knew this house. I took a couple of steps forward, as if to check my eyesight. My sight was fine; it was the house from my dreams! Literally.

I was unaware that Cate had walked back to stand by my side. It took me a few seconds to register her concerned voice. "Debra? What is it? DEBRA!"

Slowly I turned toward her, my mind like a willow tree whipping the wind. I tried to find words that would describe my emotions and not cause Cate to consider mental facilities for me. "It's one of the houses from my dreams," I began.

She scrunched her face in confusion. "What are you talking about?" she asked.

I took a deep breath and turned back toward the house. I truly had never noticed this particular house, having not spent much time in this section of town. Or perhaps it had been refurbished. But it was indeed the house from the one decent dream from the past month of nightmares. "I had one really nice house dream after Daniel died," I responded after a long pause. "This was the house in the dream!" I was glad that at least Cate knew my history of house dreams.

"Wow, that is really weird," she replied, walking to stand by me and stare at the house. "I wonder who lives there?"

33

I looked at the small gated yard, decorated with elegant outdoor art. Of course, a wind chime sang delicately on the front porch. I could see a small sign by that familiar red door but didn't feel comfortable approaching. "I don't know," I replied. "But I am going to gather up the guts to find out one of these days."

I grabbed her arm and we walked to the restaurant.

11

He comes up behind me as I wash my hair. I smile to myself, knowing what is to come. Sure enough, his hands caress my scalp, gently cleansing my hair. He cranks up the pace a bit, and accidently pulls my hair. "Careful, dear!" I admonish gently. He begins scrubbing my head harder, bringing tears to my eyes. "Ouch!" I yell, as I attempt to straighten up. But he pushes my head back into the sink and scrubs harder. I begin to scream …

Once I re-entered a conscious state and my screams receded, I knew without a doubt that I had to visit that house – it would take my mind off the horrific Daniel dream. Today would be the day to go, as it sure would beat pulling the covers over my head yet again.

It took a little time to recover from the latest dream and to scrape the kitties off the ceiling. A little canned cat food helped with the latter, though not much helped with the former. I did make an executive decision to forego the coffee for herbal tea. I dressed casually, but with intention. I wasn't sure if the house was a residence or an office, as that part of town has a mixture of both. At best, I might meet the owner; at worst, I could at least read the sign on the front porch.

I parked in the same structure as the night before, and before losing my nerve, marched right up the wooden stairs. I paused to catch my breath and admire the scene. How I love a classic front porch, with a big bright couch, wicker chairs and those perfect red geraniums. I briefly wondered why I hadn't dreamt of porches before. Shifting back to the purpose of my visit, I took in the simple yet elegant sign. There wasn't much to read; it merely stated, "William Bell" – nothing else. The font was nice, but the sign provided no additional detail in terms of what a "William Bell" is or how to reach this mysterious William Bell.

Undeterred by my confusion regarding the occupant, I walked to the door, sighing as I perused the rich red color. The coincidence of the red door did not escape me. I began the search for the doorbell and realized the door was open a crack. I stepped in before my mind could protest. The foyer was empty of humans yet filled with fascinating art objects. A bronze statue of a woman reaching out took center stage, while two large paintings of brilliant gardens seemed an appropriate setting for the lady in bronze.

I took a few steps down a hall. A man dressed in off-white leaned against a doorway at the end of the hall, staring at me. I stared right back. He straightened up and walked up to me.

"Hello, I am William," he said simply.

"Hello." I took a slight step forward, realizing simultaneously that he was a stranger, but I wasn't at all afraid. I didn't dare comment on the possible wordless conversation we might have had. "I'm Debra."

We stood silently for a time, though it didn't feel awkward. I set my radar on high and took in this tall, slender, somewhat ageless man who seemed the slightest bit familiar to me. Had I met him somewhere in town? At the hospital? That didn't seem right. I knew I would have to think more about that. His eyes were almost colorless, or perhaps they were hazel, picking up the surrounding colors. In this case, it would be cream or off-white, given his selection of clothing and the fresh paint on the walls, trimmed with natural wood. My sense of him was peacefully complicated, which was comforting in some odd way.

He seemed to take me in as well, seeming not at all surprised or bothered by this stranger standing in his foyer. It was almost as if he expected me.

"How can I help you?" he asked.

"I really don't know," I replied honestly. "My reason for being here is a little difficult to describe."

"Well that is a pretty normal set of events for me," William said with a soft smile. "Why don't you come in and join me for tea, if you are okay with that?"

I liked his sensitivity and I knew I wasn't going to leave until I knew more about this house – and the man himself, for that matter. I followed William down the long hallway. I almost giggled as I thought about touring so many houses in my dreams and here I was doing almost the same in the light of day. We entered a big airy room decorated in a variety of soft taupes and cream. Ceiling fans moved air from high above and comfortable furniture with sage and maroon pillows begged for us to join them.

"This is my office," William offered, as he gestured for me to sit down on one of the couches. He leaned his tall frame back into a huge wooden rocking chair, then turned toward a tray at his side. "Tea?" he asked. I nodded in surprise; it was as if he knew I – or someone – would be joining him. Or perhaps he had been about to have a cup of tea himself. But there were two cups on the tray.

"Do you care for rooibos?"

I stared at him, astounded. For that was the very tea I had concocted that morning to calm myself and it wasn't exactly well-known. I nodded once again.

"I think our conversation might go better if you utter a word or two now and then," he ventured, the hint of a twinkle in his eye.

"Uh, yes," I stammered. "So what is it that you do?" I took the tea and tried to get the cup to my lips without looking like I had a drinking problem.

"I am not sure you will understand, but I am a life facilitator," William replied. "I help people solve problems."

"Like a private investigator? Or maybe a life coach?" I asked.

"Well, not really, but that could be part of the full-service package," he said wryly. "It's hard to describe. I pick up vibes about problems that people have, even anticipate them, and then work on creative solutions. Then I present the solutions to them, usually long before they have articulated the problem – either to others or even to themselves. Another way of putting it is that I help people regain their power. I hope that doesn't sound too odd."

Not to me, it didn't. It sounded like a huge relief. I felt my insides release a tiny bit. "A life facilitator. I like the sound of that. Can you give me an example?"

"Well, let me see." He scratched his jaw for a moment, looking upward. "Okay, let's say that a doctor has a huge ego and a poor bedside manner. I happen to be in a situation where I observe this behavior in action, and proactively offer my counsel to better the situation – for him and all of mankind. Does that help explain it a bit?"

I looked at him incredulously. The example struck close to my frustrated social worker's heart. Given that I had a vested interest in his answer, I was compelled to ask the follow-up question. "And what was it that you did in that situation?"

William's eyes gleamed. "Well, I took him down a notch or two, but he didn't know that," he responded. "I happened to be visiting a dear friend in the hospital and made sure that she filled out the patient satisfaction survey with a blistering summary of his poor behavior. I simply helped her find the right words, then made sure that the survey was submitted to the appropriate audiences at the hospital. Then I made a point of introducing myself to him and delicately suggested that he needed some help. Time will tell if he listens."

Words escaped me. It couldn't be Dr. Evil; no, it simply couldn't. But it sure made me feel better about my own work woes. I sat back and decided to get to the point. "I guess you might be wondering why I am here."

"I am, but only if you are comfortable in sharing that."

I took a sip of tea, summoning up the courage to share my story, or at least part of it. "Well, it's a bit of an odd tale, but I am sensing that you do odd well," I said, and was rewarded with a blinding smile. "How weird would you think I am if I told you that I saw your house in a dream?"

He shifted to serious in a blink of an eye. "I wouldn't find that weird at all. There's a whole lot of weird in this world, and we need to be more accepting of it," he replied firmly.

Without a word of internal backtalk, I poured out the depressing account of Daniel's accident and my frustration at work, though I didn't go into all of the dreams. Some time – and a few tissues – later, I was able to confirm that William was truly a good listener. His eyes were intent and caring, giving me the courage to continue. Once the toxic waste in my brain was removed, I felt renewed, with a slight smidge of self-consciousness.

"How do you feel right now?" William asked gently.

"A whole lot of relieved, with a dollop of embarrassment and significant curiosity as to why I shared all of that with you, and where we go from here," I replied.

William rocked slowly; one could imagine him sitting in the chair, thinking about big problems. "That's how problems sometimes present themselves. I either see an opportunity, or one bangs on the door – symbolically or physically, as in your case. While it might not have been clear to you, you have sought my services."

"But I don't even know you!" I replied, my emotions beginning to stir.

"Yet you've told me about your strong intuition; it is no surprise to me that you would find your way here."

I sipped my now-chilly tea as I brewed a bit over his words. He made a fair point. I was well aware of my interesting gift, and given all of the dreaming, stranger things could have happened than my finding my way to William's door through the dream world.

"Okay, I won't argue the point," I said firmly. "But I still don't have a clue on how you can help me."

"Nor do I, but that's what I will be working on until we meet again," William said. "And yes, I can hear you." With that, he handed me his card, bid me a cordial farewell, and showed me the door.

"Yes, I can hear you."

I stood outside the marvelous house, staring at the red front door, recalling William's words. I had asked the question; I always do. But I was pretty sure I had imagined any sense of response in the past – perhaps someone looked at me a little differently or scratched their head. I simply did not know what to make of this new development.

I was struck by how much I had shared with William, a stranger, really. How could I sit down with someone I had never met before and spew out such bile? I remembered how much better I felt after sharing my story, but now I felt a major retreat was in order. Yet one thing was perfectly clear: William had "heard me" and that stunning development alone was enough to assure that I would be back to see him – soon.

12

What a nice house! I think. I feel a sense of warmth and caring as I enter a long hallway. An abundance of doors accent the space, all painted dark red. I wonder what is behind the many doors and I step toward the first one on my right. As I reach to open it, the radio announcer warns of thunderstorms this morning …

I woke up not screaming and smiled. My mind filled with questions about the symbolism of the doors and the similarity of the hallway to the one at William's house. It was then that I had an extraordinary insight. William looked familiar because I had seen him in a dream. I yanked my dream journal off the nightstand and flipped through the pages. Yes indeed. William was the man in the car, who started off as Daniel, and then raced down the street. I held the journal in my arms and tried to remember more of the dream. How absolutely bizarre it was that a man I had never met would appear in my dream! Even more bizarre would be to meet him after the dream, which is exactly what occurred. I reminded myself that coincidences were part of my life. As the curiosity machine in my head cranked up, I exited the bed and prepared for work, remembering to take an umbrella.

While work remained a bear, two interesting developments eased my suffering. First, though I still refused to acknowledge the coincidence of William's little example of his work, Dr. Evil had toned down his nastiness by a few notches on the nasty-meter. That eased my relationship with my suck-up supervisor. Second, I couldn't stop thinking about my meeting with William and the fact that he had surfaced in a dream without introduction. It certainly was less stressful content to ponder than evil doctors and dead husbands. I once again came to the conclusion that a person with my "gifts," if you could call them that, could be expected to have not only odd dreams, but intentional ones. I thought about William's offer of assistance. Perhaps he would be just the person to dissect the dreams with me, for the sake of a little peace at night. Perhaps, at the same time, I could put my lack of angst about my husband to sleep.

13

Ah, I remember this house! The white house, with the man in the white chair. I smile at him as I pass by. He does not look at me; he simply stares into space. As I head toward the door, I purposely look closely at his face and realize he looks a great deal like Daniel. Unlike my previous dream, the interior is completely white, barren, empty. Someone enters the house behind me, and as I turn around to the sound of the footsteps, the man who looks like Daniel lifts a large container filled with a blood-red substance and flings the contents across the room. The bright red liquid splatters grotesquely; it manages to touch every surface in the room. The man turns and looks at me for the first time and begins to laugh – a hideous laugh that echoes off the ceiling. I shake my head and step back, screaming "no, no, no ...!"

A cat's wet nose and plaintive meow interrupted my howls of protest. I opened one crusty eye to observe both cats nervously perched beside me on the bed, tails wagging. "It's okay; it's okay," I said hoarsely, doing my best to soothe all of us. I shivered and wiped my eyes, still feeling the horror of the dream, particularly the awful look and laugh of the man who had such an uncanny resemblance to my dead husband.

"What the hell is this about?" I muttered to myself. I forced myself to write down what I remembered of the dream, pondering the disastrous shift my dreams had taken over the last few weeks. Somehow, I didn't think this was a natural approach to grieving, but what did I know about it? I thought once again about William Bell. I swung my feet out of the

44

bed. Yes. It was time to talk to William. I desperately needed some advice.

Arriving a few minutes late to work, I tried to call William, but realized that I didn't have a phone number or an email for him. Looking him up on the Internet proved fruitless; Google had him at the top of the search, which didn't surprise me. But the lack of detail was mystifying. It simply said:

William Bell
www.williambellbeing.com

"He must have paid a boatload of bucks for that website address," I grumbled, as I clicked on it. A clean white web page opened instantly, and I couldn't help but notice the contrast of the bright red lettering:

Please visit when you are ready.
William Bell

I felt frustration bubbling up from deep within. Actually, it seemed a far better emotion than the fear, anxiety, and sadness of recent days. I hung onto it as I went into a staff meeting with my insipid leader, stewing over the website message while pretending to hang on her every word. Who would invite anyone who visits a website to come on over? It couldn't be meant for me specifically; I mean things don't work that way. I doodled fiercely on the meeting agenda. And by the way, no "contact us" box was available for address information. It was a conundrum.

"Are you still with us, Debra?" asked Carol in her syrupy, fake voice. "You seem so distracted, dear. How are you doing?"

I hung onto the lifeline of my frustration and gritted my teeth, hoping it looked something like a calm smile. "I am fine, Carol, fine and dandy. I'm taking a few notes here."

"I see," Carol replied. "Remember that we are all about team here, and we need you in the game."

I smiled my gritted-teeth grin and nodded. Carol brought the meeting to a close and we scampered away like chipmunks. God, I *hate* this woman, these people, this job, I thought as I bolted down the hall. The intensity of my emotion surprised me. When did I start hating my work? I had always wanted to help people. But there it was – a raging, dark disgust with all matters work. I would have to store that observation for further reflection because it was time for me to seek out William Bell.

The late afternoon sun setting on an early spring day found me on William's porch, with sunlight dancing on the walls. I took a deep breath, thinking that it might have been the first breath I had taken all afternoon. It felt good, but intense emotions were still spinning in my depths. Before I could knock on the door, William opened it and said, "Welcome. I have been expecting you."

My eyebrow rose slightly as I looked at him, unsmilingly. William looked at me questioningly. "You were coming to visit, weren't you?"

"Yessssss …" I managed to respond, the yes sounding like a hiss. "I still don't quite understand how this works."

He smiled reassuringly. "I get that a lot," he replied. "Let's say I have an understanding with the cosmos. Would you like to come in?"

He held his arm out while holding the red door wide open. I sure had seen my share of red doors lately – another notion worth exploring at some point. My head felt as if it might explode. Soon we were in William's wonderful office, and I felt a smidgeon of angst depart my insides. Our last session certainly was helpful; I had come to peace with sharing so much with a virtual stranger and had a weird sense of optimism. Perhaps this meeting would produce some positive outcomes as well.

He poured the tea, which, of course, had just been prepared, then waited for me to begin, which was problematic, as I didn't have a clue where to start.

"It's my dreams," I said finally. "I didn't mention them when we met last. But they are getting very disturbing. I know they mean something, and I am sure it's probably related to grieving, but I have got to do something about them."

"You mentioned that you had seen my house in a dream," William replied, looking at me intently.

"Yes, well that was the last truly decent dream I had," I responded. I opened my purse and pulled out my dream journal that I had remembered to grab that morning. "Here. I write down my dreams and I thought perhaps you could take a look." I stood up, handed the journal to William, and walked over to the window. Somehow, the view into his backyard reminded me of an Arizona dessert, which seemed impossible during March in Michigan. The use of stone and unusual evergreens, accompanied by stunning bronze sculptures, reminded me of Sedona, a peaceful, spiritual place for sure. I sighed and turned back toward William's sitting area. He had not moved a muscle. I frowned, as I expected he would have had his nose in the journal by now.

"Aren't you going to read it?" I asked.

"Of course. But it would be helpful if we could discuss a couple of other items first."

"Like what?"

"Like your husband and your work."

My frustration raised its head a bit further inside of me.

"We talked about that last time," I said slowly, with great emphasis. "This time I want to talk about my dreams."

William put the journal down, leaned forward, and lowered his long arms onto his knees. "You seem to be under the impression that I am a psychiatrist or something," he stated politely. "But, you see, I am not. I know it's probably not at all clear how I can help, and yet you are here, so I will try my utmost. I will read your dream journal, but not right now. What I really want to know right now is about your deep love of Daniel."

I stared at William, rendered speechless. The most sickening feeling wrenched my gut as I chewed on his words. My deep love of Daniel. My deep love of Daniel?

"HOW FUCKING DARE YOU?" I said in an unexpectedly harsh tone. I didn't use the F-word much at all, and it felt surprisingly appropriate at this moment. I quickly realized that I had hit crisis-mode – I had revealed way too much to a total stranger, who somehow knew more about me than I had revealed. It was as if a swirl of dark emotion descended upon me. I continued, my voice escalating. "You say you are not a shrink and you have the audacity to want to know about my most intimate feelings? Is that what a 'life facilitator' does, dearest William Bell? Messes with people's minds with the pure intent of facilitating a positive outcome?" This last part came out sarcastic and shrewish, but I was not coming down to Mother Earth anytime soon.

"Screw you."

I grabbed my purse and literally ran out of the room, down the hall and out of William's beautiful, peaceful house.

14

I am driving on the highway. I am late – so very late – to work. It's raining and, of course, every single car has slowed to a micro-crawl. I have five minutes to make the meeting with Carol and Dr. Evil, so they can tell me again how wrong I am. I grope around the passenger seat to find my phone; perhaps I can make a quick call and push back the meeting. I look back up. Oh my God, there is a man in the road – he's standing right in front of my car. I can't stop in time. I've hit him, run over him! The noise of the car hitting him is the most awful sound I've ever heard. Wait, there is a worse noise – he's screaming in pain! He's calling my name. It sounds like ... Daniel! I stop the car, grapple with the seatbelt and bolt out of the door. There he is, bleeding profusely, his arms and legs at impossible angles, his kind, normal face battered. He keeps screaming "Debra!" as it rains harder and harder. Blood runs off his body and forms puddles around him. I fall to my knees beside him. "I am so sorry! Daniel, I am so sorry!" I shriek. I try to hold him in my arms, but he keeps slipping away. I am covered in blood. He's dying, and I killed him.

Suddenly, I realize a man is kneeling next to me. He puts his hand on my shoulder. "Debra," he says quietly. "You are dreaming. Please hear me now."

I look at him, this tall, calm man, close at my side. He looks so very familiar. I look at Daniel again, who has stopped screaming. In fact, he's not even bloody.

"Debra," the man repeats. "It's a dream. You have managed to gather all your worries into a nightmare of epic proportions.

Let it go; let yourself wake up. When you wake up, know that you have some work to do."

He stands up and walks away. I look down once again at Daniel. He is no longer there.

Slowly, very slowly, I opened my eyes, one at a time. They felt painful and swollen. I moved one leg, then the other; it was as if I'd overdone the exercise and my muscles were screaming "time-out." Following the physical assessment, I reluctantly shifted to the mental side of things, knowing full well that I was doing my utmost to block out the absolute horror of the dream. Yes, I remembered it in amazing clarity and detail. Where was the soothing skill of allowing bad dreams to fade quickly in the morning light?

The only part that remained fuzzy was the end of the nightmare, where some stranger spoke calming words to me. It truly helped, but I couldn't quite capture the scene in my foggy brain. I shook my head as if to eradicate the awfulness and questioned whether I could even attempt getting out of bed. But I knew I had to get to the hospital. Today was going to be one of those banner days. My presence had officially been requested at a pow-wow involving Carol, Dr. McCrory and a representative from Human Resources. That didn't sound good at all. But I was ready to state my piece, and the opportunity to promote the idealistic concept of doctors actually being nice to their patients was enough to propel me out of the bedroom. Dissecting the nightmare would have to wait until the evening. But I knew I would suffer through the hangover-like symptoms that resulted from it all day long.

It became quickly apparent at the hospital that my idealism was for naught. Walking into the meeting, I had every sense of walking into a gunfight in a bad western. Dr. Evil sat at the head of the table, with something resembling a smirk on his face. The HR representative had her face turned downward, writing furiously. Carol, obsequious as always, jumped up and provided an awkward welcome. "There you are, Debra! Come in, come in! You know Melody from HR, right? She will be sitting in on our meeting today."

Clearly, they already had started the meeting and I didn't have to guess the topic. I sat down warily. They started in on their scripts: "Debra, we know that you have had a difficult time with the death of your husband," Carol began. I stared at her coldly. "But the purpose of this meeting is to formally suggest that a sabbatical might be appropriate for you at this juncture. Dr. McCrory continues to be concerned about your overzealousness with regard to patient care and his supposed lack of empathy."

Dr. McCrory nodded sagely. Melody, the HR rep, kept writing.

"Unfortunately, you continue to cross a line, and we have discussed this several times now," Carol carried on. "We've conferred with HR and while in normal cases we would start a performance evaluation process, we are willing to hold off on that to see if a little R&R doesn't do the trick."

My mind tuned out the sound of Carol's shrill voice as she began to tick off a litany of travesties on my part, all having to do with supporting patients in their greatest time of need – my view, of course. Then it happened. I heard a distinct "snap" in my mind, resulting in a large roar. The roar grew louder and louder and I could feel my blood pressure rising – fast. I feared for what would come next, because I was pretty certain it wasn't going to be pretty.

Then, the voice of the stranger from my dream returned.

"Debra ... Let it go, let yourself wake up. When you wake up, know that you have some work to do."

That soothing voice faded away, as did the loud roar. I looked around the room and Carol was still talking. No one had noticed a thing. But all the fibers of my being were in alignment. I had some work to do and all I had to do was wake up and tackle it head-on. The time was now.

I stood up, interrupting Carol in mid-complaint. "I have something to say," I stated in a strong yet calm voice. "I quit."

Before Carol could open her mouth again, I walked out of the room, though I did take a tiny peek on my way out, hoping to see a look of consternation on the evil wonder's face. I was rewarded for my efforts.

I headed home and immediately called Cate. Fortunately, she wasn't flying some organ somewhere and answered her phone. "Where have you been?" she asked. "I haven't talked to you since you found that house. What's new?"

I was tongue-tied for a moment. So much had happened, I didn't know where to start. I quickly decided on an organized approach: "Four things: The house was awesome; I met a crazy dude who calls himself a life facilitator; the nightmares got really bad, and I quit my job."

No surprise, dead silence ensued from Cate. I took the opportunity to take a deep breath and then realized I wasn't ready to pour out my troubles, even to my best friend. As she began sputtering about the state of Debra, I interrupted, not for the first time that day. "Cate, I know I have a lot of explaining to do, but let's meet for lunch tomorrow. I realize that I'm not ready for this conversation right now. But I am okay, and I will give you the blow by blow tomorrow."

Another pregnant pause commenced, followed by a sigh

loud enough to be heard clearly over the phone. "You better feed me well," she said. "It's going to be a long lunch."

I allowed myself a hint of a smile. "It's a deal. Let's talk tomorrow."

I hung up with Cate, glad that I had at least established contact with her. I hoped that I would be ready to talk to her the following day, but I had a lot of reflecting to do in the meantime. The enormity of my actions had not sunk in yet, and I struggled to maintain the calm and clarity from the conclusion of the awful meeting, as I determined what to do next.

I stalked around the house, refilling the cats' water bowls, putting a stray dish in the dishwasher and sighing heavily. If I wasn't still ticked at William, I would have considered calling him. It also belatedly occurred to me that I had used some pretty strong language when I stormed out of his place. Damn. I also remembered that I still didn't have a phone number for him. Damn again.

Okay, I thought. Let's take an inventory. I made a cup of tea – yes, rooibos – and sat down in my cozy living room. My husband died fairly tragically a few short weeks ago. My dreams began to go from nice to nasty in a hurry. Work went from patient-focused and productive to patient-averse and poisonous in about the same amount of time. I swore at a very nice, calm man. I quit my job. I simply needed to find a Zen-like therapist who could look at me peacefully and say, "And how do you feel about all of this?"

How DID I feel about all of this? I put down my cup and sat back in my funky chair. I felt like I wanted to explode; that is how I felt. "There, dear therapist: Do you have your answer? Now get the hell out of my living room!"

Did I say that aloud? Well, if the quick exit of the cats was any answer, I must have. I shook my head. I simply didn't know what to do with the cacophony of emotions and events from the last few days. I did have a brief release when I remembered that calming voice in my dream, and then in the meeting at the hospital. How incredibly strange. Then, a final insidious thought entered my brain as I noticed dusk settling in outside. I still had to face going to sleep.

15

The warm water feels so marvelous as it makes its way down the back of my head. Soap suds flow into the basin below and gentle fingers massage my temples. One cup of warm water, then another, then the words I often hear: "There babe; it's all done." I slowly raise my head from the sink and turn toward the waiting towel. "Daniel," I say softly. "We need to talk."

I had survived the night. While emotions continued to crawl around my nerve endings, I knew that something had shifted in me. Several thoughts emerged simultaneously. I didn't have to go to the hospital this morning because I had quit the day before. I had to see Cate and catch her up. And I had to visit William Bell.

Lunch with Cate took considerable time, thanks to my promise to share everything that occurred, and the amount of food Cate needed to give her the energy to listen. Fortunately, our enduring friendship and Cate's emergency training allowed her to take in my strange tale. She, too, appeared fascinated by the calm voice of my dreams. "What do you think that is about?" she asked while munching on an onion ring.

"I am starting to form a theory," I replied. "I can't help but think that William Bell has something to do with this. As you know, we didn't part well after our last little session."

Cate wiped her mouth, though it could have been that she was disguising a smirk. "I can't believe you, of all people, swore at him. You never swear."

"Well shit. Shit. Shit. Shit."

"You sound like Colin Firth in 'The Kings' Speech.' He didn't swear either, though it did seem to help his stuttering."

I almost grinned. "Well, my next stop is William's office. I have some questions that need answering."

I purposely did not want to contact William in advance to let him know I was coming over, not that I had a phone number. It seemed unnecessary, and that was confirmed when he met me on his porch.

"I suspected that you might visit," William said in greeting. He peered down at me with what looked like genuine concern in his strange gray eyes. "I was a bit concerned when you left here, but I didn't think it productive to track you down. You had some business to attend to, I believe."

I stared at him. That was more monologue than I had heard from him previously, with a bit of emotion to boot. He gestured for me to follow him inside. This time, however, we didn't go to his fascinating office. "I want to show you something," he said, and led me up a staircase of epic proportions. A series of intricate circles, almost impossible to describe, were carved into the wood bannisters. I typically would have asked about them, but I was too busy trying to figure out William for the hundredth time in the last many days. Questions fired off in my head: How much should I tell him? What might he know about the voice in my dreams? How could I apologize for my poor behavior the day before? What is upstairs that could possibly be of benefit right now? I followed his tall frame up the impeccably polished steps.

William made an immediate right at the landing, opened a maroon door, then proceeded up a second stairway, this one a narrow set of winding stairs. I felt short of breath as I journeyed upward.

He paused at the top and held out a hand. "I'm sorry for the hike, but I believe you will find it's worth it in the end," he said, ever-pleasant.

I took his hand and let him give me a boost up the final steps. I looked around in silence. I knew the house had a cupola, but I hadn't paid much attention to it in my previous visits. First, it was round, not square, with a series of arches and floor-to-ceiling windows. Huge candles in glass pillars occupied the center of this sizeable space, with handsome wicker chairs and soft pillows in an abundance of colors.

"Please, have a seat," William said, releasing my hand and pointing to the nearest chair. This time, no hot tea awaited us, but I still had a strong feeling that William knew I would arrive at his front door when I did. "I come here when I am working on a problem, or when I need to do some creative brainstorming. There's something about being up in the air in candlelight that appeals to my mind."

He took a seat to the right of me and I waited for him to continue.

"This is where I came after you left our meeting in such a hurry. I needed to think about things. And this is where I was when you dreamt about Daniel."

There is no way that William could know that I had suffered such a nightmare involving Daniel. No way at all. Once again, a blazing hot rage ignited low in my belly and started to race toward my heart and my head. For once, I didn't stare dumbfounded at William, but turned away, desperately hoping to regain some small degree of composure.

As the inner battle continued, I gazed at a painting on the wall. The art in the room had not registered when I entered; now I could take in four huge, vibrant pieces outside of the four arches. If one stood in the right place, each arch served as a natural frame for the painting. Using exploration as a method to manage my emotions, I took in the first painting. Butterflies of all colors filled the canvas, so exquisite and delicate that they almost looked like they were dancing right in the room. Butterflies dancing around a red door. My mind immediately linked with my recent dream about butterflies.

"Debra …" William began, but my immediate raising of a strong hand toward his face halted the counsel that was to come. My eyes flitted to the next painting, of a stark, stone room. And to the next, an odd contemporary visual of a series of hallways. The fourth and final painting was of William's house, just the way it revealed itself in my dream. Each and every painting represented one of my recent dreams. The fire inside abruptly burned out and I put my face in my hands and began to sob.

The wailing went on for some time, and as it finally began to lose momentum, I heard William's deep voice. This time, I found myself ready to listen, though I remained crouched in the huge cozy chair, with my head tucked under my arm.

"Debra, do you remember our conversations during your first visit?" he asked.

A guttural affirmation struggled out of me from within.

"I don't mean the 'hellos' and 'what a lovely house,'" he continued. "I mean the real communication."

I knew what he meant, and I knew why he was bringing it up. After all the years of asking people whether they could hear me, he was the first one to say, "Yes I can hear you."

"Yes, I can hear you," William repeated. I felt his hand touch my shoulder. I peered up, through swollen, wet eyelids. "It should really not be much of a surprise, then, if I hear other things about you as well."

58

I digested this for a minute, as I gave myself the gift of a deep sigh. My extreme anger vanished instantly, and an epiphany took its place. It wasn't anger that boiled inside of me. It was fear, plain old fear, disguised by anger. My social worker self laughed at my inability to see that reality sooner. The next aha followed quickly: I had spent most of my life trying to be normal, and while I occasionally checked in mentally with people, I never expected an answer. Then I got one – from William – right in the middle of a terrible series of crises that would shake anyone to the soul. Yet, I had failed to acknowledge that he might have a similar gift. I pulled myself together and sat up.

William sat straight in his chair, his arms on his knees, having the look of a little boy who knew he had gotten into trouble, and was ready to confess his sins to get back in my good graces. Frankly, it was pretty endearing. That was an interesting notion in its own right. I shook my head to get back to the matter at hand. William began what sounded like a confession.

"I've always been able to read people. I get ideas about things, sometimes very strong emotions about situations. Unlike you, I was encouraged by my parents to honor the gift, and I have tried to do so. I wasn't lying when I described myself as a life facilitator, though I do hate the term. I try to help people accomplish their dreams, address an issue, survive a crisis – in a variety of creative ways. I know people think I'm a bit strange and I am okay with that. I show just as much as needed, to get the job done."

He paused, seeking reaction from me. Finding none, he continued, with a slightly anxious look.

"I will say I've shared more with you than I've shared with

anyone. And now I am going to do something that pains me to do, but I think it's the right approach. I am going to leave. I suspect you have some thinking to do."

With that, William Bell headed down the stairs.

16

I must have dozed off in William's amazing cupola, because I am pretty sure my snoring woke me up. Not surprisingly, a comforting male presence sits across from me, gazing at the painting of the butterflies. As I stretch, he turns to face me, and to my utter shock, it's Daniel. Dark emotions of shock, fear, and guilt bind inside me as I try to find my voice.

Daniel puts his finger to his lips. "Shhh ... " he says comfortingly. "It's okay. I know you want to talk to me. I'm here."

My head clears a tad, and I remember my last dream. "Daniel – dear – I've so failed you," I begin. As he tries to respond, it is my turn to put my finger to my lips. "No, let me continue. While I loved you, I never loved you with passion," I confess, my voice wobbling a tiny bit. "I tried to be something I was not. I put away the real me, and pretended to be a loving, normal wife. When you died, I did a pretty darn good job of torturing myself for those failings."

Daniel leans back in his chair, folding his arms and sliding one leg over the other, as I had seen him do a hundred times. "I know that, dearest Debra," he responds. I stare at him, dumbfounded, as I seem to be doing a lot these days. "I knew you were special the minute I set eyes on you. And while we are confessing things, I knew you had some interesting aspects and I couldn't handle that. So I simply pretended that you were a nice, normal wife. That wasn't fair to you. I'm truly sorry."

My eyes fill with tears, though my dark emotions eased. "Where do we go from here?" I ask.

Daniel grins and stands up. "Why don't we stay in touch – in your dreams? But promise me that you will have nicer dreams about me than you have had in the last few weeks. Okay?"

With that he was gone.

I must have dozed off again in William's stunning cupola because I jumped out of the chair, my gaze whipping toward the butterfly painting and back to the chair beside me. Daniel wasn't there. I rubbed my temples with a vengeance, realizing that, yet again, I had dreamed. I eased back into the chair as I realized that the dream had been … okay. Better than okay. Cathartic came to mind. A brand-new emotion emerged, one I hadn't felt in a very long time. Hope, perhaps. I realized I wanted to find William and debrief this new development. He probably already knows, I thought, snorting gently. Much like one does after a bad fall, I checked in with myself. No broken bones. No broken anything.

I headed down the stairs. I was sure he would be waiting for me. But much to my surprise, no William hovered at the bottom of the second staircase. It was dusk now, and I could see a soft light coming from a room just off the foyer, in the opposite direction of William's office. I headed toward it, walking into a large, airy room, perhaps originally a living room. But this room had lost its living room roots. It looked more like a homey museum of contemporary arts, with one exception – a modern office set up in a striking bay window in the front of the room.

There was William, placing a sizeable bamboo plant on the teak desk, next to a sleek laptop, a tea mug with a cat on it and a book suitable for a coffee table entitled "Dream Houses." My rusty inner sense began to slowly crank up.

"What's going on?" I asked with great calm and poise.

"I think you know," William replied with a twinkle in his eye. "You need a job and I need an assistant. I've been 'advertising' for help for some time, and you are the one who came to the door. I simply thought you were answering my 'ad' when you showed up on my porch."

I stared – yes, again – at this fascinating, quirky man, realizing there were many more layers worth exploring. With a great burst of cosmic energy, I knew that it was unnecessary to provide him with an update from the cupola, and I realized with every fiber of my being that I was supposed to work with William. He simply grinned.

"What work would I do?" I finally asked, then put a hand over my mouth. "I just remembered that we haven't discussed how I pay you for your facilitator services!"

William's eyes twinkled. "First, I have no idea what you will do," he replied. Then, without saying a word out loud, he offered a follow-up statement: "But oh the fun we will have figuring that out!"

"And second," he continued aloud, "I have always had an issue with getting paid. Perhaps I can work on that – with your assistance."

"I accept the offer," I said formally, then burst out laughing, as I passed back a few musings of my own.

Reader –

Can you feel my incredibly deep sigh of relief? That was a tad tougher than anticipated. I must confess that I was somewhat unnerved when Debra's tortured dreams of killing Daniel emerged. My, that woman can go dark. What a mind. I've never taken a client to the cupola before; that is my private space. But it seemed the right place for a major breakthrough. I don't quite know why she became so emotional about my art collection. Time will tell, I suppose.

While that office set-up has been awaiting the right person for some time, it was quite the insight to tempt her with a new opportunity – premature perhaps, but it will help solidify her healing. As her gift emerges, she will be a tremendous asset to my work. My heavens that was a good lark.

Ready for another one?

—William

SAM

Hello again dear reader!

Now, let me introduce Sam. I met Sam via pure happenstance, though pure happenstance doesn't really happen with me. Does it with you? With anyone? I digress. An intense gentleman seemed in a tither in a coffee shop, where I was innocently sipping tea and pondering a problem facing one of my clients. That's ideal coffee shop work, don't you think? He blasted through the door and ordered a great big cup of caffeine – apologies, but I don't speak latte-grande-whatever. In the very brief time I was there, he was back at the counter twice more.

Hmmmm … Why did I care? Well, he intrigued me on some level, which does happen on a frequent basis. Why was I intrigued? What caused me to take a pause? I have concluded that it was his computer. He clearly was waiting for someone, and he kept opening up his computer, then crashing the lid back down again. Certainly, that can't be good for a computer! On his second irritated trip to the counter, I mildly commented on his repeat visit for coffee. I even introduced myself. He seemed like a nice man – a little self-possessed, but not off the edge. He looked at me oddly, but I am used to that as well. I brightly offered up the insight that it appeared he was stood up by someone. That caused a stir. A face does tell all. I simply suggested that he put his computer to good use and record what was going on around him. So straightforward, really. But if you believe in trite old adages such as frying pan to fire, you will find a bit of both in Sam's story.

—William

1

JANUARY, COFFEE BUZZ SHOP, BIRMINGHAM, MI

9:15 A.M.

God, I hate winter. It's freezing inside and out. Here I sit, waiting for some pompous ass to come in and interview me. He's late. It's been 30 minutes. Do you wait for a possible employer as long as a tenured professor? I can't remember the rule anymore. I'm giving it an hour and then I'm giving it up. I need a job, but I can't imagine it makes sense to look wimpy and stay longer than that.

9:40 A.M.

This place is jammed. Why are all these people socializing at a coffee shop at nearly 10 in the morning? Don't they have work to do? There's the steady in and out traffic of long-haired blondes getting their non-fat, no whip soy lattes with their cell phones glued to their heads. There's the moms with their enormous baby carriages, desperately seeking adult time. What have they done to baby carriages in the last few years? They look like frickin' flying saucers, some of them. As I look around, there are all sorts of meetings going on … what an odd place to hold a meeting. It's so noisy. What's with the dude near the counter? Okay, so I've been up there a couple of times; I'm bored out of my mind, so I might as well indulge in a few cups of coffee. He looks a little peculiar, for sure. He told me his name is William

Bell. How he stuffed those long legs under these tiny tables, I'll never know. He offered these stupid tips on writing. What business is it of his? So, I am writing. WTF???

9:45 A.M.

I am pissed. This jerk isn't coming. I don't want to look lame and call him up. I'll send an email when I get home and cheerfully suggest that I must have messed up the time – fall on my sword. I'm not sure I even want that job. It's bad enough to get laid off from the ad agency, but to take a job hawking coupons simply sounds pathetic. Yeah, I've got to pay the bills, but I've got to come up with some other prospects. What a crappy market. There's gotta be more to life, for God's sake! And I've so gotta to start writing again – that would be the ticket. Wow ... check out all of the gotta's in this paragraph. That tall guy left a minute ago, smiling at me like he knew something. Weird.

9:50 A.M.

I'm leaving in 10 minutes, I swear.

It's funny – I've gotten hooked into the most interesting conversation behind me. I would have stereotyped these two women as rich, stay-at-home moms, but they are doing some big business deal. Who would have thought it?

10 A.M.

Okay, maybe I'm not leaving. I can't believe I am getting intrigued by this place. There's a whole bunch of stuff going on here. I've never been much of a fan of the coffee shop scene – seems like you can suck down a ton of coffee and pay tons of money for the privilege. But there's a vibe here. The *two dames have concluded their business deal — involving big chunks of change. Now, a guy and a gal took the table, and I swear they are discussing his divorce. Maybe she's an attorney. It's amazing what you can pick up in here.*

10:15 A.M.

Well, still no visit from the asshole, big surprise. But I'm getting my energy up in this place. A group of high school girls just came in, must be on lunch break or something. Talk about people-watching, wow! I think I'll start coming here every morning, take in the scene, see if it compels me to get writing. Until tomorrow.

2

Sam Taylor packed up his laptop and stomped out of the coffee shop, still stewing over being stood up, but less bristly thanks to the intrigue he had found in the rather contained but lively quarters. He brushed back his slightly-receding cropped hair as he unlocked his beloved Saab 900. "I sure hope I can keep this little baby," he muttered to himself as he folded himself into the driver's seat. Dark clouds continued to brew in Sam's brain as he drove home to his apartment and headed in the door.

He surveyed his palace through the lens of the newly-un-employed and sighed heavily. What a drag, he thought for the umpteenth time that week, again rubbing his head, an unconscious habit derived from stress and intensity. Beacon Advertising had laid off nearly a quarter of its creatives more than a month ago, and even with that sizeable reduction, Sam still couldn't believe the company could do without him. It took a solid two weeks for him to even get up the energy to find his resume, let alone edit it.

It had been a depressing few weeks. Usually on top of the world, Sam kept wondering if his turning the magical age of 40 had anything to do with his demise. He had it all, he thought: Great job at a great company, money in the bank and no weights around his neck in terms of dependents. He lived a fulfilling life as a single male; he purposely chose to reside in an apartment, rather than bother with a mortgage, and his parents were happily living it up in retirement land in Florida. He knew he was attractive to the women he dated, but they knew full well that he wasn't the marrying kind. Nope. Not him.

He had stayed busy, of course; the job was more than full-time, keeping him at the office for a good 10 to 12 hours each day, and with his brain remaining on the job for more than that. In his spare time, he worked out – one must keep up one's muscle tone, of course. He showed it off to an array of attractive females who were more than willing to have dinner or attend local sporting events with him.

In rare moments, he would sit down at his computer and see if the beginnings of a novel might erupt from his fingers. His brain constantly entertained fascinating ideas about potential plots, but something always halted the process of translating them into the written word. He could imagine all sorts of reasons for his habitual procrastination.

His big birthday was low key – a gathering of pals at the sports bar with a bunch of beer and a few gag gifts. He hadn't gone apeshit that night but the next day, if he was at all honest, he did have a niggling feeling, a very vague sense of discontent. Loss? Boredom? More beer than he remembered? He shook it off, went on a five-mile run and returned to his efforts to create the perfect ad campaign for powering up a new electric car. One week later, BAM. Job over. We love you, man, but this climate is brutal; we got a fresh new idea from another creative … yada yada yada. His 20-year career as "Sam, Sam the Creative Man" had imploded.

Sam paced around his apartment, which seemed to have grown much smaller recently. He knew he needed to send a simpering email to the jerk who had stood him up, but smartly figured he'd better cool off for a while. He considered going on a run, but it was so damn cold outside. He grabbed a sandwich and sat down in front of the television. "That's another thing," he stated fiercely to his TV. "Daytime television sucks." He didn't even bother to turn it on, but let his mind wander back to the coffee shop instead.

Frankly, he was amazed at the bevy of emotions the morning had drummed up: his annoyance at being stood up, and, if he was honest with himself, the whack it took to his already sagging self-esteem, as well as his intrigue with the people in the coffee shop. He had never paid attention to the goings-on in a coffee shop before. To sit and listen in for a while, well that was more interesting than expected.

Then there was the guy, the one sitting by the counter. William Bell. What a wild card he was. So tall, kind of elegant and out of this world. It's like he could almost read minds. He definitely felt some curiosity about the fellow. Sam finished his sandwich and burped his semi-gratitude. He stood up and headed to his study to send the email to asshole and get his resume out to a few more sites.

3

JANUARY 30, COFFEE BUZZ

9:30 A.M.

Well, I'm back at the Buzz again. At least this time I am not waiting for some jerk to come in. No tie today, thank God. That's an improvement for sure. It's funny. It seems like my radar is up today, wondering what the place will be like. Will it be the same as yesterday, or will it be different? I can't imagine it being very different. I'm starting to wonder what I was thinking yesterday.

9:45 A.M.

Guess who's just walked in the door? It's that guy. Man, he has such a look to him. He nodded as he passed by my table and I swear there was a twinkle in his eye — like frickin' Santa Claus or something. A very skinny Santa to be sure. He ordered some funny herbal tea. Now that makes sense, doesn't it? Who comes into a coffee shop and gets tea? I sure don't get some people.

10:02 A.M.

So here's something interesting. The exact same song played at the exact time today as yesterday. What was it — yeah, Bob Marley! Love that dude. And at the same moment, the same woman walked in the door as yesterday. What a coincidence!

Sam closed the computer when the tall man walked over to him and held out a hand. "Hello Sam. I'm William Bell," he said. "I briefly met you yesterday."

Sam stood up and shook the outstretched hand. "Hey man, it's nice to see you again," he fibbed, surprised that William had remembered his name.

"You seemed a tad frustrated yesterday, Sam," William remarked.

"Yes, you certainly sensed frustration; I really hate to be stood up."

William offered a knowing grin. "Given how casual you look today compared to yesterday, could I wager a friendly little bet that it was a job-related no show?"

Sam felt his insides prickle a bit. "Yes, you'd sure win that wager," he replied in a somewhat fake cheerful voice. He waited for William to reply, but he only stared at him. "Sadly, I'm out of work right now, and was truly ticked when my first interview didn't pan out."

William handed Sam a card. "Perhaps I can be of assistance. Why don't you drop by or drop me a line sometime?"

Sam looked down at the pristine white card with its simple message:

William Bell
www.williambellbeing.com

"And what is it that you do?" Sam asked, still grasping for insight from the card.

"Ah, I am a life facilitator of sorts," he replied. "I try to help make things happen."

Sam looked at him curiously. A life facilitator? he thought to himself. What the hell is that? But before he could come up with a politically-correct comment, William Bell patted him on the shoulder, said "good day!" and headed toward the door.

4

Sam returned to his apartment, which seemed to have shrunk yet again. It didn't take him long to set up his computer and head to williambellbeing.com, given his growing curiosity about the lanky fellow at the coffee shop. Why was he not surprised that the home page looked remarkably like his business card? He clicked on the name "William Bell," and to Sam's surprise, a message appeared: "Hello Sam. Welcome to my website. If you are interested in my services, why don't you stop by my office this week sometime?" That's all there was. No flash intro, no links, no drop-down menu, no contact information. "William's font choice is nice," he grudgingly thought to himself.

Sam scratched his jaw as he considered the optics of the website message. How could he do that? He must have taken a look-see at my computer. It was too difficult for his mind to wrestle through, so he started to close the browser. Before he could click the button, a second message appeared. "You will need my address: 450 Arrow Avenue, Birmingham. You will know it when you see it." The browser window closed as Sam quickly grabbed a pencil and scribbled the address on a nearby scrap of paper. Too bizarre, he thought, as he leaned back in his chair, hands behind his head. Way too bizarre. But he sure was going to drive by the place as he couldn't think of anything better to do with the rest of his day.

Sam grabbed a quick handful of peanuts and a diet cola, then headed out to his car. Downtown Birmingham was practically a stone's throw from his apartment – 15 minutes max. The town was sort of a mixed bag – partly snooty old money and partly trendy new money. Office buildings mixed with fussy stores and coffee shops abounded – including his current favorite. Anyone with a caffeine addiction would not get the shakes in downtown Birmingham, Sam mused. It sure sounded like a successful ad campaign to him.

He turned onto Old Woodward, and sure enough, he knew William Bell's office the moment he saw it. Amid the gynecological offices, women's stores and the ever-present coffee shops, one eccentric Victorian house-turned-office stood proudly on the corner, down the block from Coffee Buzz. Of course, he had seen the building, but as there was no sign out front, Sam hadn't known much about it. But now he was pretty darn sure it was William's place. He swung into an open parking space on the street and took a closer look. To call it Victorian, after a closer scan, was misleading. It was Victorian Modern. Is there such a thing? he wondered. Probably not, but that's what it looks like.

It was as if two eras crashed together uncontrollably, like the old commercials about chocolate and peanut butter, resulting in something better altogether. There was his ad brain getting cranked up again. The Victorian front porch battled pleasantly with the large glass bay windows; the gables clashed with the vibrant red paint and the picket fence fought against the modern water fountain in the front yard. Somehow, it all worked – brilliantly.

Sam couldn't help himself; he eased out of his car and headed up the front porch. He had no intention of visiting today, but his curiosity was getting the better of him. As he stepped onto the porch, he paused, listening to the pure sound of wind chimes hanging from the ceiling. Again, it was as if two worlds collided when a deep voice said, "Welcome. I've been expecting you. By all means, please come in."

There was no one there, of course, and he couldn't even find a speaker among the chimes. It was a cordial welcome, so Sam shrugged his shoulders and opened the door.

Sam stopped in his tracks in the front foyer. The array of large historical displays and modern car art rattled his senses. William ambled in from a neighboring room. "Welcome Sam!" William began, looking deeply into Sam's eyes.

"Uh, thank you," Sam replied awkwardly. He made a brief mental note to stop feeling awkward. He tried to look at William, but he couldn't tear himself away from the view. Much like the outside, the interior of the building began to show its eclectic self. The immediate effect of discordant art had shifted to include what he could only describe as early American – like "go west young man." An enormous wooden wagon wheel hung suspended from the high ceiling of the foyer. "What's the wheel about?" Sam asked.

William gazed upward as if surprised by the sight of the wheel. "Ah yes," he replied thoughtfully. "You would see the wheel early on, wouldn't you?" He stared at Sam once again. "It's a symbol of life, of course."

Of course, it's a symbol of life, Sam thought. He could imagine that this place had more symbols of life than even over-achieving marketers would include in any campaign.

William put his hand on Sam's shoulder, silently suggesting that Sam follow him into the next room, where more eye candy awaited. The room had been a living room at some point in its past. Now it appeared to multi-task. At the far end of the room, a series of exhibits suggested an artists' gallery or reception space. On the side, several incredibly comfortable-looking chairs surrounded a small, contemporary fireplace. Nearest to the French doors they had entered sat an efficient-looking woman at a wooden table with the bare essentials – two folders, a few pens, a laptop much nicer than his, a mug, a plant. Somehow, the different areas of the room didn't combat one another; the effect was eclectic but peaceful. Sam's eyes returned to the woman at the table; he was sure that she winked at him.

"Sam, I would like you to meet Debra Kelly, my office manager." She stood up, holding out her hand, while William continued. "Actually, we are still trying to figure out her title, and already I am thinking it won't be 'office manager.'"

"Greetings Sam, and welcome," she said with a laugh. Her eyes sparkled and she had an old soul look to her, Sam thought. He had the funniest feeling that she had said something else, very quietly. He shook his head and smiled at her.

"It's nice to meet you as well. I have to confess, I'm not quite sure what I'm doing here," Sam ventured.

Debra's hazel eyes twinkled some more. "You are not alone! William has that effect on people, and his office does the same. I'm sure you two will find plenty to talk about."

She sat back down and turned her attention to her computer.

William steered him back to the foyer and down a long hallway. At the end of the hallway, William paused.

"You must be writing about what you see," he offered complacently.

Sam blinked, but couldn't think of a word to say in reply.

William then opened a massive door and invited Sam in. It was clearly William's private office and special space, and if Sam had thought the rest of the building interesting, this room was positively mind-blowing.

Once again, the word "clash" came to Sam's mind as he stood in the doorway, taking it in. The room was sizeable, of course, with its ceiling playing active duty in the design effort. Wheels of all shapes and sizes swung from overhead perches, on what must be pretty damn strong wiring. "This takes the concept of wind chimes to an entirely new level," Sam observed. As he looked around, he noted a design theme of circles. Literally everything in the room was circular in some fashion – chairs with round seats, circular tables, even the art on the walls, creatively framed. Sam gasped as he took a few steps into the room.

William smiled and followed him, offering him a seat.

"But how …" Sam began.

"It wasn't that difficult, actually," William replied. "We practiced the same principles you find in nature, and le voila. I guess I am pretty fond of symbols of the meaning of life. But let's get back to our previous conversation."

Sam couldn't remember the previous conversation and looked at William with consternation. William smiled again. "As I said, you must be writing about what you see."

Sam pulled his attention away from the room and thought about the perceived drivel from the coffee shop and quickly blew him off. "Yeah, that's what I'm doing, alright," he replied. "I'm writing about the richness of life."

It was not the most sensitive of replies, particularly for a first meeting. But William simply smiled his quirky smile and nodded.

"What it is that you do again?" Sam said rather brusquely. "You said something about a life facilitator, whatever that is?"

Again, a small smile preceded William's words. "My

profession is hard to explain," he said. "I use the phrase 'life facilitator' because frankly, I can't seem to come up with a title that explains it any better. I guess Debra and I will continue to struggle on the title front."

William leaned forward and continued. "I provide life support – no, not that kind of life support. I provide support through life's challenges and hurdles – both work and personal. And no, I am not a life coach, counselor or shrink. The best phrase I can come up with is 'life facilitator,' as I told you.

"Let me elaborate, as I sense a tad of confusion on your part. I tend to defy the general approach to work. Rather than being hired by a client or a company to do something, I get a strong sense of a person or a company and their needs. It can be anything from someone going through a personal crisis to an interesting new product idea. I work to address those needs, then offer up a solution to the potential client. I know it sounds a little backwards, but surprisingly, most give me a big thumbs-up and off we go."

Sam was more than confused; he was dumbfounded. "You mean you create work products and pitch them to a potential client?" he asked. "All I can think of is an advertising guy crafting a commercial for Chevrolet, then contacting the Chevy general manager or advertising director and saying, 'here, buy my ad.'"

"Something like that," William responded.

Sam probed for sarcasm but felt none. "It doesn't work that way in the real world," Sam said knowingly.

"Yes, but it works that way in my world," William said quickly, with a funny little smile. "But you are not the first to have some question on what it is that I do."

Sam failed to find an appropriate response so decided to shift the conversation. "Okay, so why am I here?"

William leaned even closer to Sam. "I am offering you a service."

"What service?" Sam asked.

"I just told you," William replied. He abruptly stood up and moved to the other side of the room, where a potting stand clearly served as a desk.

Sam rubbed his head in frustration. He leaned back in his chair and stared once again at the natural riches around him. What kind of man creates such a space and what kind of man can afford it? he wondered to himself. What service was William offering?

William returned with a book in his hand. "Here, why don't you borrow this?" he offered. "It's a good friend of mine, and it might be insightful to you."

The book was battered and worn. "It must be a 'good friend,'" Sam said wryly as he reached out for the book.

"No need to review it here; just take it and we can discuss it further at our next session," William said. He stood up, indicating that the meeting was concluded and walked Sam out the door. Before he knew it, Sam was heading to the coffee shop, book in hand.

5

JANUARY 31ST, THE BUZZ

3:45 P.M.

Well, big surprise; here I am again, with my computer and arsenal of coffee. It's my first afternoon at my new home away from home. Not much has changed from the morning view. I am surrounded by little groups of women gossiping over their lattes. I suspect they are about to hustle out of here to get home before their little kiddies get off the bus. The big corner table is occupied by a large group of ancient men talking about God knows what in God knows what language. I bet they have a pretty regular routine here. Now, students are trooping in. How lame is this!

3:55 P.M.

The noise level is insane. Between the screeching noise of the coffee-making process and the fake cheerfulness of the staff, everyone in here has ratcheted up the volume. I can hardly hear myself write. What was I thinking? Screw this.

He stopped writing and his mind shifted to what William shared at their meeting. *"You must be writing about what you see."* He allowed himself a small snort as he took a swig of coffee. "What I see is all of this drivel around me," he hissed.

Sam pulled out the tattered book that William lent him. Alfred Hitchcock's *Rear Window*. It was written by a fellow named John Belton. Sure, he knew the movie; who didn't? But he'd never heard of the book nor its author. He flicked through the pages of the worn book, wondering why this particular book would be so well-loved. He thought about the movie, the intensity of Jimmy Stewart and the uniqueness of the plot. He returned to his computer.

4:03 P.M.

Sure it's an awesome movie, of course. Jimmy Stewart was perfect in the role and so was Alfred Hitchcock for that matter! How could anyone create a movie about a guy with a broken leg who sits in the same place for most of the movie? The guy is wheel-chair-bound for heaven's sake! The outside scene never changes and, yet, is always changing. Hmmm. That's interesting.

But what has this got to do with me? I do have an urge to watch the movie again, of course. The back of the book is interesting: Voyeurism and dreamlike fantasy?

Sam stiffened, then bent over the computer, typing like a fiend.

4:05 P.M.

"You must be writing about what you see." A giant lightning bolt has struck me between the eyes this very moment. William wasn't making a casual observation. He was making a suggestion, or more of an imperial command, perhaps, delivered in that damn neutral, almost fussy, tone of his. All of a sudden, I have a completely different context. I remember my change of tune yesterday about what was going on in this place. Today the Buzz seemed back to its old

self, but a minute ago, things started to change again. Did I see a passing of notes from one of the high school skirts to an intense fellow heading out the door? The old guys in the front corner, still arguing about God knows what, seem to have their rheumy eyes focused on a car outside the shop. What's that about? And what is it about the music? It's almost as if there's a code ...

I'm typing like mad here, as my mind spins out of control. Am I going nuts or is something really crazy going on? I must write what I see. I must write what I see!

Sam typed up his observations for a few more minutes, then packed up and headed home. He unlocked the door and the same quiet, messy space stared back at him. Greasy dishes were stacked high by the sink. Papers remained a staple on practically every surface. It was so quiet after the racket at the coffee shop that it seemed foreign to him.

He realized how weary he was. It had been quite a day. Sadly, he hadn't forwarded his search for a new job whatsoever.

"Damn, damn, damn," he muttered to himself. "What am I thinking?"

6

With fierce resolve, Sam attacked the following morning with job-seeking fervor. Two hours later, he leaned back in his creaky office chair, ran his fingers through his hair, and blew out a deep breath. He mentally checked off his progress: four requests for LinkedIn recommendations, six new contacts, four applications sent off to prospective employers, one Netflix search for "Rear Window", a pity purchase of a couple sci-fi novels (used) on Amazon.com and a furtive list of questions to explore when next at the Buzz.

"Coffee! What a great idea," he rationalized. "I need a break after all of that work."

Fifteen minutes later found Sam seated at what had become his normal table in the matter of a few short days. As usual, the place was jammed. He belatedly remembered that it was Saturday; the weekend had arrived, and he hadn't felt its onset whatsoever. That's depressing, he thought as he pulled out his computer.

A large bony fist came into his line of view, slowly knocking on the table. "Knock, knock," said the fist – or rather one William Bell. Sam looked up, feeling a new regard for the distinguished fellow.

"Good afternoon, William!" he said brightly. "Join me for a coffee? I'll even buy."

William sat down, carefully folding his long legs under the small table and placing his environmentally-correct travel mug in front of him. "Already have my tea – my favorite – vanilla rooibos," he said cheerfully.

Sam didn't even take the bait. He knew William was going to be an herbal tea drinker, and he knew full well that if William Bell said his tea was vanilla rooibos, then it was vanilla rooibos, whatever that was.

"It's a velvety, smooth, calming tea," William replied, clearly reading Sam's mind. "It's grown in South Africa."

"I'll remember that for next time," Sam said blithely, before shifting quickly to what was really on his mind. "I am glad to see you, actually. I've been thinking about what you said to me yesterday."

William sipped his tea, his gaze unwavering and unreadable.

Sam felt uncomfortable but carried on. "I came back here, and I realized that I was misinterpreting your advice. You said, 'You must be writing about what you see,' which I took as a petty observation."

William chuckled.

"But you were really offering some counsel, weren't you? I must write what I see. I looked around at that point, and I started seeing all sorts of interesting things."

"Really?" responded William, taking a long sip from his mug. "What did you see, Sam? Do tell."

Now Sam felt ill at ease. He leaned back slightly. "Well, uh, I saw things differently here. I'm not sure I can articulate it well. But I guess I'd say that things shifted for me, and I'm eager to explore that a bit."

William stood up and held out his hand. "Well carry on, then! I'll see you at 10 on Monday at my office."

He swiftly and efficiently headed out the door, managing to avoid the next round of coffee enthusiasts coming in the door.

Sam didn't even get a goodbye in. He also quickly noted that he hadn't arranged to meet William at 10 a.m. on

Monday or any day for that matter. He laughed to himself and shook his head. It was time to take in the scenery.

Sam began a slow assessment of his current coffee house of choice. Now, there was so much to see. First, the table of senior gentlemen: Were they friends or just old fellows who needed a purpose each day? It was clear that they had an agenda; the question was what sort of agenda did they have? They were animated in articulating their views on some topic, complete with arm-raising, table-banging and frequent trips for more coffee, with the logical follow-up visit to the bathroom in the back. What was it that they were talking about? They were fascinating to watch in action. All had been around the block more than a few times in life and had the faces to prove it. Their passionate debates truly must give them a reason to get up each morning, he thought to himself. Unless it is deeper than that …

Sam's eyes shifted to the next table, filled with the latte ladies, all dressed in their daily uniforms of tight yoga pants and North Face jackets. Forcing his eyes not to roll, he tried to listen in on the conversation. A few words and phrases floated upward like caption bubbles: "tickets to the event," "what to wear," and "oops, gotta get to yoga!" He shook his head and opened his computer, avoiding a mental diatribe on the opposite sex.

1:48 P.M.

Ran into William again. I actually told him that I was sensing a different scene here, and he didn't laugh. He looked somewhat pleased, almost like a teacher whose student has made a small modicum of progress. What a weird dude!

For kicks and grins, I'm going to let my imagination wander – what better to do on a surreal Saturday, really? The testy

*testosterone bunch in the corner: What are they really up to?
What if they are plotting something? Who would know? They
sure aren't speaking English. It could be code for something.
Or maybe they are pretending to be angry old dudes – maybe
they are secret agents. That's it!*

*And the lovely ladies – are they really all heading to yoga?
Or did they task the one who frantically had to get to yoga
with some assignment? Maybe they are a gang of women
who take revenge on the opposite sex. They get hired by some
hysterical female, whose husband is an idiot who can't keep
it in his pants. They quietly take care of the problem, with
a little education and persuasion. No one would ever know
that these hens are actually a wily gang of men abusers.*

The computer slammed down – for the first time this day,
Sam realized. Who was he kidding? What possessed him to
think that there was something odd or serious going on in
here? He stood up to start loading his computer into his bag,
jostling a departing customer.

"Excuse me," Sam said, looking up.

It was one of the elderly fellows from the corner table,
shuffling toward the exit. "No problem," he replied, in perfect English.

As he continued to make his way to the front door, the old
man dropped what looked like a folder paper.

"Hey – sir – you dropped something," Sam blurted out,
moving forward and reaching down to pick it up.

In lightning speed, the older man inserted his body between the paper and Sam, grabbed the paper and efficiently
transitioned out the door. There was no shuffling involved
this time, nor a word of thanks.

Sam stood and stared, as the man started to power walk down the street before disappearing around the corner, looking more like a marathoner than an octogenarian. Turning back to his computer bag, Sam rubbed his chin thoroughly. Maybe there is something going on here after all, he thought. Just maybe.

7

No surprise to Sam, he found himself standing on the front porch of William's incredible office on Monday morning at 10 a.m. sharp.

Debra opened the door immediately and welcomed him in with a big smile and hello. "William is not here yet, but I can get you a cup of coffee, if that would ease the wait," she said.

"That would be great," Sam replied.

"Come on along; I'll show you the wildest coffee room you have ever seen."

Debra took Sam down a hallway he hadn't seen during his previous visit. They entered a room, if it even could be called that, which was absolutely circular in its design, not surprisingly. There wasn't a flat wall or corner in the space. Sam looked questioningly at Debra, who laughed aloud.

"Yes, it was one of William's projects," she said. "He is always creating something; this was going to be a new physical structure for teams to encourage innovation. But it was an epic fail: Who knew that walls and corners are actually useful structures in an office setting?"

Sam slowly looked around. It was like a Dr. Seuss book of opposites. Curvy walls. Straight lines of appliances extending out to the middle of the room. Lights in the floor, rug on the ceiling. Windows along the floor. It certainly helped explain the creativity of William's fascinating office space.

Debra watched Sam, understanding quite well the difficulty of getting one's arms around William and his personality.

Sam turned with unanswered questions in his eyes. Before he had a chance to pose an inquiry, Debra began to speak.

"His profession is somewhat difficult to explain," she began, as she pulled out a coffee cup for Sam. "I know because I ran into him unexpectedly awhile back and it took me a long time to figure him out. He is one of those genius types who probably suffers from adult attention deficit disorder.

"William started his business at least 25 years ago, with an interesting approach. He picks his clients, not the other way around. I'm sure he told you that. Or he gets fascinated by some obscure project and sells the concept to a company. Even more surprising, the company or client generally love the ideas he offers and pay amazing sums of money for the pleasure of doing business with William. Why? Because he provides results, even though they can come across as unorthodox at times – many times. Frankly, it's crazy."

Sam found himself yet again scratching his head. "What is his business, exactly?" he asked.

"Hmmm. That is a darn good question. It's not quite marketing and it's not quite business consulting. Let's call it creative problem-solving with a twist: William selects the problems. He combines a dab of strategy and a dash of some combination of energy and intuition, then develops something with an approach that would make no sense to the average person, let alone a business person. Somehow, he creates an amazing outcome, time and time again. Don't ask me how he negotiates his pay; that remains something of a mystery to me."

Debra paused; it seemed she was struggling with whether to go deeper.

"Can you give me some examples of his work?" Sam pressed.

"Well yes, I can. He helped me personally through a pretty big crisis. When I know you better, perhaps I will tell you a little bit about it. But be assured that if someone had told me that I was about to embark on a journey of discovery involving dreams and the deceased, I would have thought them certifiable. So that's the people side of things."

Sam didn't know what to say about that, so simply nodded as Debra continued.

"Oh, here is a good business example! A few weeks ago, he pitched a television ad to a local advertising agency. They absolutely loved it. Had he ever created a television ad? Nope! But he got the idea one night and came in raring to go the next morning."

Sam began to feel a tight pressure in his chest. The conversation was eerily aligned with his somewhat abrupt departure from his agency. He shook his head slightly. There couldn't be a connection, he thought to himself, while attempting to smile nonchalantly at Debra.

"I mean it was wild," she continued. "How would William know anything about electric vehicle batteries?"

8

With the precision of a surgeon, Sam opened his computer and began to type.

10:48 A.M.

What the fuck!

He delicately shut the lid of the computer, then crushed his coffee cup. Fortunately, he had consumed most of the coffee immediately upon receiving it, burning his tongue a bit, and only a few drops of coffee splattered on his pants and shoes. "Fuck William Bell!" he raged to himself.

After Debra's bombshell, he gracefully excused himself, claiming a forgotten appointment. He was quite proud of how calm he had been, but she didn't look persuaded at all; she looked concerned. In fact, now that he thought about it, she had an eerie quality of seeming to know more about him than he had shared, much like William himself. He couldn't get out of the building fast enough, sure that William would magically appear at his side on the front porch, with some peaceful statement about Zen or Karma or something. But he hadn't shown his passive ass, and that was probably a good thing.

Rage building, Sam decided he couldn't stay at the Buzz. He packed up his computer carefully, knowing that he could easily smash it into oblivion at this moment in time. As he once again pondered the possibility of William magically appearing at his side, William did just that.

"Hello Sam! I am so sorry I missed you this morning," William said with great cheer.

Sam was rendered silent, as his brain hosted a debate of epic proportions, the right side voting for a quick punch to William's face, the left suggesting a mature dialogue instead. While the debate continued, Sam zipped the computer bag and walked silently to the door.

"Allow me," William said brightly. "I have another piece of counsel for you, Sam. You must be writing about what you feel."

That was it. Sam could feel every single hair on his head slowly begin to rise, much like a sports car powering up. What a chintzy throw-away line. Feelings? Yeah, he'd share his feelings. Sam raised his arm, clenched his fist, then slowly and methodically unclenched each and every finger. He would not deck William Bell. That would be going too far. Sam's right brain continued to pitch for a fight, however, and it was all he could do to manage the inner battle, so he remained quiet.

William seemed absolutely unperturbed. Was he unaware of what he had unleashed, Sam wondered, or was he stoking the fire on purpose? Another wave of fury crashed through Sam, and this time he couldn't hold it back.

Sam grabbed William's arm – hard. "Look, asshole," he hissed. "You don't know anything about me! My career, my writing, my feelings are PRIVATE. Do you get that, you twisted creep?"

It was William's turn to remain silent. Sam searched William's face for a reaction. Did he dare to smirk? Did he have the balls to actually smirk at me? It wasn't an easy face to read but at this point, it really didn't matter.

Sam twisted the arm that he still gripped as he tried furiously to come up with a sentence of great authority. "Leave me the fuck alone!"

He pushed William away and took off down the street.

11:30 A.M.

I am so incredibly pissed off. I have to notch it back a few for sure because I am a little bit out of control. Deep breath. Okay then, let's see what we have here. I was compelled to find a new coffee shop, given that my Buzz has been poisoned. This is a new place, like the 13th coffee place in downtown Birmingham. I guess we have a caffeine problem in this community. It's called The Mustard Seed. What a sappy name. Just as sappy as vanilla rooibos, right? Don't GET ME STARTED!!!!!!!

Fuck, now I am screaming at my computer.

Sam groaned, sounding more like a boxer preparing for the next round. He looked around at the quiet shop – it clearly hadn't been "found" yet by the coffee crowd. It has character, unlike the chain places, Sam ruminated, taking in the rustic décor and the real fireplace. Only a few of the tables were occupied, and it was nearing the lunch hour.

11:42 A.M.

That man knows jack shit about me. "I have to be writing what I feel" – what a bunch of crap. That sounds like it's right from a bad novel. Hah, I made a little joke, yeah? What the hell am I doing with my life? Why am I sitting in coffee shops creating conspiracy theories about average Joe's? And why am I letting myself be lured into the web of William Bell?

Sam interrupted the beginnings of his pity party when the very same elderly gentleman, who power-exited the Buzz a couple of days ago, ambled through this coffee shop door. This time he was definitely not the old shuffling soul who debated life with his kindred spirits; this time he appeared to be on a mission. Looking quickly around the coffee shop, the man briefly set piercing dark eyes on Sam, looked away, then returned to check out Sam more carefully. Sam casually looked back, trying to appear uninterested. After a couple of seconds, the man's eyes moved on, and he exited abruptly. Sam's fingers couldn't connect with the computer keyboard fast enough.

Okay. Something is going on. Who is this guy? I feel like he's some double agent or something. Hey William! Check this out! I'm FEELING! Ha! That really was a good one. But something is going on and I am going to have to use some of my limited free time to check it out. And I think that guy recognized me. I can FEEL IT IN MY BONES! Ha!

Sam, amused at his reflections, felt the rage-o-meter slip down a couple of notches. He started to think about how to approach this newly-emerging dilemma. I have to go back to the Buzz tomorrow to see if this guy is at his regular table, he thought to himself. With that decided, Sam's thoughts slithered back to the events of the morning, particularly his conversation with Debra. He had enough self-awareness to know that his ego had been struck a sizeable blow, the cause for most of the poison he felt. But there was more to it. Once again, Sam opened his computer.

God I'm angry! I can't imagine how I've managed to meet the guy who took away my job. Okay, not directly, but how in the hell can a regular guy walk into a big ad agency and offer up an actual ad for electric vehicle batteries? Who the hell does that? NO ONE! Who would even agree to see him? And what was so special about his ad? Hell, my temples are throbbing; I can't get my arms around this at all.

He took a few deep breaths. Slightly calmer, Sam sought his inner maturity and asked himself one of the big questions.

What was it about William's ad that thrilled those goons? Why was it better than what I've been working on?

Sam slumped in his seat, crossed his feet, and looked out the window. He started to experience some new emotions beyond anger to the nth degree. He reluctantly let in envy with a dollop of anxiety and let them feed for a while.

Okay, here goes. Let's try utter honesty. I haven't been doing my best lately, and deep down I know it. So what if I'm not thrilled beyond measure by electric batteries and some of the other client work I've done? Like groceries. Really? If I had to look at one more photo spread of vegetables and come up with pithy descriptions of them, I think I would have started throwing them at the photographers. I know that. I get that. And I get that I'm pissed because they got rid of me before I got rid of them. But damn William Bell – what the hell does he know about electric car batteries anyway?

After significant spewing into his journal, Sam observed that his rage had diminished, but his annoyance with William remained. Ironically, he noted that he had written several pages on his feelings. He couldn't begin to understand what was going on with regard to William – and most of his life right now. Grudgingly, he acknowledged to himself that change was required and wrote one more sentence in his journal.

Maybe it's time to figure out what I want to do with my life …

Sam turned off his computer and headed home.

10

Heading toward the Buzz the next morning was not as painful as Sam expected. He thought he might pick up the remnants of the emotions from the day before, and he certainly wasn't in the mood to run into William. Frankly, more than anything, it was his curiosity around the old man, who might be morphing into a spy, that led him back. On the way to Birmingham, Sam created a mental list of the many characters who wandered through the Buzz during his many visits there. He wanted to see if he could detect any connections among them. And he was going to pay close attention to the big table in the corner.

To Sam's chagrin, it was closed. A roughly-written note was taped to the door: "CLOSED DUE TO SMALL KITCHEN FIRE. WILL REOPEN VERY SOON."

"Well isn't that odd?" said a voice behind Sam. Sure enough, there was the wonderful William. Sam hadn't put William on the mental list he created while driving into town, so he was caught without a pithy retort. Sam quickly observed that William would love the phrase "pithy retort." Sam also took a second to check in on his emotional state. He found little of the rage from the previous day, which he viewed as progress. After a small but not unmanageable pause, Sam offered a "Well, I guess it is."

"This certainly wasn't on the news this morning," William replied, moving to Sam's side. "I would have thought I would have heard the sirens. Something is amiss."

Sam managed to avoid a little sneer at William's choice of words. "I guess I'll head to the Mustard Seed. I visited there yesterday, and it works."

"May I join you?" asked William. "Or is it too soon?"

A small spark ignited in Sam's interior, but extinguished itself quickly. "No, you can join me, but please know that I've got things to do," Sam replied in a firm voice.

"No problem," William replied brightly. "It will be interesting to see which of the Buzz regulars have made their way to another coffee place. And I only need a couple of minutes of your time."

They entered the cheery coffee shop together, and unsurprisingly, the place was nearly filled to the brim, compared to the quiet of yesterday. Sam's head quickly whipped to the big table in the window, and sure enough, the crew of older gentlemen reigned supreme, with his friend the spy engaged in some hefty argument in an unknown language. Did his eyes dart quickly toward Sam and back again? Sam wasn't sure.

While Sam surveyed the scene, William had somehow managed to find an empty table. Sam got his roast java and joined William, awaiting what he assumed would be an awkward pause. But that was not to be the case.

"I am glad I ran into you, as I owe you a huge apology," William began. "I was so intrigued with your career situation that I failed to comprehend how difficult it would be for you to learn about my first efforts with advertising."

Sam quickly sipped his coffee to get his dropped jaw back in place.

"You see, these things just come to me. I guess I'm a tad impulsive, but when I have an idea that appeals to me, I act on it quickly. I do hope you can forgive me."

As Sam tried to pull his muddled thoughts together to respond, a large crash interrupted his brief reverie. Sam's spy man had knocked a plate to the floor – probably while gesturing wildly – and a nearby yoga mom sprang up seemingly to assist. Sam held his hand up to William and drank in the scene playing out in front of him. Yoga mom picked up the unbroken plate and put it back on spy man's table, as he slowly rose from his chair, waving his hands in the air and motioning his thanks. Sam drilled in on the plate, and sure enough, a small piece of paper was slightly visible underneath it. Sam exhaled loudly, then whipped his head back to William, so he wouldn't get caught staring.

William was not staring at the plate debacle; he was staring at Sam.

"You saw something. What did you see?" he asked in an uncharacteristically impatient tone.

Sam did not answer. He slowly took a sip of coffee, contemplating the many possible responses he could make to William on a host of items, while maintaining an eye on the pair across the room, who were now moving into lightweight comments such as thank-you, it's okay, all the best. Yoga mom was packing up to head out the door and spy guy seemed to be making his way to the bathroom tucking something into his pocket. Sam absolutely knew that something big was happening and that he had to find out what. He put down his cup and stared right back at William.

"Thank you for the apology, William. I'd like to talk more about that, but right now, I need to take care of a little business."

11

Sam took a deep breath and marched into the men's bathroom. Like most coffee shops, the john was not exactly spacious, with a stall and two urinals. The stall was occupied, suggesting that spy man was "engaged." Sam leisurely tended to some business, then took his time washing his hands. As he was about to depart, lacking anything else to take care of, the toilet flushed, and the door opened. Unfortunately, a non-descript corporate type emerged, tucking his Wall Street Journal under his arm as he headed to the sink. Sam quickly headed out and spotted the back door by the restrooms. "Shit," he said to himself, as he returned to the table.

William looked up with great interest, but Sam tried to play the "business as usual" card and sipped his now-cold coffee. This made William stare that much more at Sam, saying nothing. No surprise to either of them, Sam couldn't take the intensity and broke the silence.

"You are going to think I'm insane, but I think there's some shifty business going on between some of these coffee types," he said. "I've been watching some of these folks for days, and I'm seeing some wild things."

William leaned toward Sam. "Tell me more."

Sam poured out all that he had been observing in the coffee shop, particularly the suspicious activity with the elderly gentleman. William listened intently, hands folded, elbows on the table. "I tried to track down spy-guy in the john, but there's a back door to this place and he's gone,"

Sam concluded. "It sounds so lame, but my gut tells me that something is not right."

"It's a bit like 'Rear Window,' isn't it?" William said after a short pause. "And why not? So what are you going to do about it? Dare I ask how you 'feel' about it?"

Much to Sam's surprise, he found himself smiling. "I 'feel' more alive than I have in a long time, to be honest. I'm itching to do some writing."

And write he did. Sam stayed at The Mustard Seed for the remainder of the day, long after William departed with a second cup of tea in his new Mustard Seed environmentally-correct coffee container, with the phrase "have a little faith," on it. After updating his journal, Sam opened a new document and began writing down every single thing that had happened in both coffee shops since the day of the failed interview.

Now and again, he reverted to his journal to note insights.

God it feels great to be writing; I can't believe I let this slip away. I feel good right now. My mind is cranked up with this insane coffee house business and I am thinking it might make a good story. I can't decide whether to stick my nose in all of this crap, but I sure can write about it. Who knows? There may be more drama if I keep looking out my own rear window.

That William dude. What a piece of work. You could have blown me over with a feather when he apologized. I can't get over it. Then I tell him the whole weird-ass story of these coffee crazies and he doesn't blink, merely asks how I feel, and for once I don't feel like punching him. He is the strangest fellow. I almost feel like he's nudging me toward these new possibilities. There's that damn word again. I guess I am feeling some things. Crazy.

On to more serious things: Could I make it as a writer? Could I write a compelling piece of fiction (or non-fiction) about these coffee shop capers?

Sam slowly closed his computer and gazed out the window. Much to his surprise, it was late afternoon. He glanced around the coffee shop, which was now fairly empty of java fans. A lone attendant cleaned up behind the counter. The obligatory community table sat empty. He blinked his eyes a few times and whipped open the computer once again.

I just realized that I've been in here for hours and it feels like no time has passed at all. I've been so damn focused on this drama and writing it all down was incredible. My energy is sky high. I feel … great.

Sam shot out of the coffee house, shoving his computer in his bag as he walked. He needed to talk to his new-found career advisor.

12

The day was waning as Sam hustled up the street to William's place. The setting sun caused a southwestern hue to fall over the house, making it glow. While certainly on a mission, Sam paused and took it all in. He shook his head in amazement and took the steps two at a time. So much had changed since he had departed the place in such a pissy fit a day before.

He hadn't called ahead, and he didn't care. He knew William would be there. And he was right. William met him at the door, clearly expecting him. He held two cold beers in his left hand while his right reached out to shake Sam's hand.

"Have you ever tried a 'Hoppy Ending Pale Ale?'" William asked with a smile. "It's from Palo Alto Brewing Company. I love selecting beers based on their names; it's such a delightful pastime. I haven't tried this one yet, but it seemed the right one to share with you."

To his credit, Sam took in a great deal right then – his lack of surprise that William was waiting for him, William's incredible outburst of beer facts and, of course, the fact that any beer could be truly named "Hoppy Ending." He grinned at William as they strolled down the hall to William's incredible office.

A short minute later, they were settled in chairs and clinking beers. Sam felt that this as a much better scenario than being pissed beyond measure – in the angry sense of the word.

"Tell me what's on your mind," William said.

Sam did – over the course of a couple of beers, an incredible sunset and brilliant appetizers that seemed to appear out of nowhere. He started at the beginning and did not spare much detail. When the data dump was complete, Sam slumped over – weary, but surprisingly relieved.

William had not asked one single question, nor showed much emotion at all. He simply listened. When Sam was finished, he took a sip of beer and leaned back.

"A sad tale indeed, Sam," he said. "It truly breaks my heart when I find someone who has great talent but leads a miserable life."

Sam started to bluster about it being not that awful, but William waved him off. "I could see it immediately, Sam," he continued. "You looked like a lost soul in the coffee shop when I first happened upon you. The amount of anger you demonstrated during our little mishap seemed more about discontent and frustration – but at least you were showing some emotion.

"You see, so many people aimlessly wander on this planet, without portfolio, without passion and purpose. Oh, don't get me wrong. Most are busy beyond measure, working hard, leading full lives of oh so many things. But they aren't doing what they want to do, finding out what makes them sing. You have been one of them – busy ad exec, hot dates, life the way you supposedly wanted it. Now you have been shaken out of your comfort zone, and you admitted to yourself that you really weren't that happy and carefree. Sam, you have been given a gift."

Sam nodded wryly. That certainly was an understatement.

"Now you have the chance to make a change. You even have a solid glimpse of what it is that you really want to do. The next question is whether you have the balls to do something about it."

Once again, Sam wasn't offended in the slightest, though he was surprised that William knew how to use "balls" effectively in a sentence. William was right. He stretched long and hard, then looked straight at the very serious William.

"Thank you. I have much to think about. And more to feel." He clinked his empty beer bottle with William's, stood up, and strolled out the door, wondering if indeed he had the balls to do something about it.

13

Sam headed home, surprisingly peaceful. He smiled as he observed his lack of angst – a word William would use for sure. He felt like he hadn't been to his apartment in days. And the old pad looked it. Through the eyes of someone who was seeing life a bit differently, he took in the emotionless, colorless, treasureless place he called home. It almost made him physically ill. Growing restless, Sam wasn't sure what to do next – rip the place up? Cancel his lease immediately? Because, of course, he didn't own it. Cool dudes want to get up and do something new and different when the urge hits, right? Not that he'd ever done that in all the years he had called this shell home. Sensing a possible pity party about to come, Sam quickly found a bottle of scotch and poured a tall one over rocks – not to dull his senses but to sip and think.

His sipping and thinking took many hours. When he struggled to find the bedroom, long after midnight, he had the beginnings of a plan.

Sam returned to the Buzz the next morning, which had magically reopened. This time, he needed the coffee more than the stimulation of the morning's attendees. But he was a man on a mission – several missions in fact. He opened his computer to fine-tune his musings of the night before, but before he could type a word, the big table in the corner lured him in. There he was – the spy. Sam couldn't believe it. He jumped up without thinking and marched up to the table, getting into the spy's space. The old men looked up, startled at the interruption, and with questions in their eyes. They began to babble in a different language, spy man right with them. He was only a little old man, looking fearfully at Sam. This confused Sam; he knew what he had seen the day before. When he was about to back off and apologize, he saw the tiniest glint of amusement in the eyes of said little old dude, almost taunting him. Without thinking, Sam lunged.

All of the men began to yell, some whacking Sam around the head. The usually slow coffee team arrived very quickly and hauled Sam away from the table. While the table clucked in horror, Sam was told that he needed to leave the Buzz and not come back. Within seconds, he was out the door, computer in hand, coffee missing in action.

How quickly the newly-peaceful reflective Sam transitioned into enraged Sam. There was only one place he could think to go, one person who knew the whole story. Off to William's he went, grabbing a last glimpse of the table in the corner, imagining the passionate retelling of the travesty the frail elderly man had endured.

William was not there. Debra wasn't even there. Sam sat on the porch with computer bag in hand, drumming furiously on it. Logically, he knew that he was out of control. But dammit! This guy was getting away with something and he knew it. As he allowed his emotions and his thoughts to escalate, up the stairs of the porch came both William and Debra, who apparently had gotten coffee themselves.

They smiled at Sam, bantering about The Mustard Seed, which they cheerfully described as their new favorite coffee place.

Sam cut through the banter by abruptly standing up and very formally asking William if he had a few minutes to spare. William appeared quite surprised, apparently taking in the fact that this was quite a different Sam from the night before. He looked at his watch, as if to suggest he had something better to do, then shook his head and smiled at the seething Sam.

"Of course, Sam; do come in," William said pleasantly, and they headed to his office. "Do you need a coffee?"

Sam did not reply. He merely took his seat from the previous night and waited for William to sit down. Quickly and urgently, Sam updated William on the events at the Buzz. He was pleased that he had thought to come straight to William; he would have some ideas on how to address this spy issue and the fact that he was now persona non-grata at his home away from home. Sadly, Sam failed to mention his deep reflection from the night before.

William's face underwent an amazing rapid transformation from peaceful to thunderous, which Sam was at least successful in diagnosing as that of someone who was truly enraged.

William quickly confirmed that powerful observation. "Why you stupid little ass," he said with a quiet almost hissing voice. "I give you my best counsel – and some damn good beer – you leave last night with a mission, and in a few short hours you've gotten yourself kicked out of a coffee shop for being aggressive with a little old guy!"

Sam appeared flummoxed. "But I told you all about the spy last night."

William cut him off. "You told me what a miserable human you are," he bellowed. "You told me how much you loved writing. You told me about your passions and your dreams. You sure didn't mention the need to stereotype people who are different from you, you biased little shit!"

Sam's brain tried to take in angry William and simply bailed. "But the spy …," he began and then stopped.

That was all William needed. He stood up, opened the door to his office and yelled, "Get out. You've had your 'Rear Window' moment. Forget writing what you see and feel; you just need to write! Go write the damn ending to your story!"

Tail between his legs, Sam headed down the hall and out the door. Debra was furiously typing as he departed, yet he had a sense that she had heard – or sensed – everything. For once, Sam had no agenda, not even a coherent thought about what to do next. His brain remained in neutral as he walked down the street.

It was a long walk. Ever so slowly, Sam's brain began to function again, taking very small steps toward analyzing the state of things and figuring out what to do next. Sam somehow avoided the natural tendency to skewer William with blame and feel victimized himself. He even managed to acknowledge William's perspective on Sam's muddled priorities. As he thought more about it, he felt his behavior was truly awful, regardless of whether the old man was a spy or not. Further, the spy stuff was getting in the way of what Sam really had to figure out, and that was his future. What was his purpose now?

Several circular miles later, Sam landed at The Mustard Seed. He really did like the atmosphere, rationalizing his permanent removal from the popular Buzz. He removed his computer bag from his now-aching shoulder and pulled out his faithful computer. But rather than journaling, he started a new document and titled it "Rear Window: A Plan of Purpose & Passion." He appreciated the irony of the view from the rear window and dared himself to use such bold language as he began crafting a brand-new start to his life.

14

It was three long months before Sam saw William again.

Much to his extreme surprise, Sam had accomplished a great deal of his plan. He converted his living room into a writing studio and installed exactly one piece of art on the wall – a poster of Jimmy Stewart in "Rear Window." He thought long and hard about pulling out of the lease, but finally decided it wasn't prudent at this time. He simultaneously applauded his lack of impulsivity, then impulsively and impatiently wished he could move somewhere else. Not yet, he reminded himself, not yet.

The living room proved to be a better office than his tiny, cramped office down the hall. He left his creaky chair and the many plaques and advertisements there, keeping the door closed on the past. Cranking up the writing process was difficult, but he persevered. He kept his Internet and email shut down, to avoid his ego-fueled tendencies to see what was happening at the ad agency or network with old buddies in hopes of finding a new gig. He truly knew that he had to give writing a serious try. And he avoided the coffee shop scene, for oh so many reasons; perhaps the biggest reason was to avoid running into William Bell.

As the weeks passed, Sam crafted a draft of a spy novel from his journal and notes and entitled it "Coffee Shop Spy." Long hours of writing peppered with a myriad of emotions of defeat, accomplishment and anxiety finally produced a fairly-decent first effort. The ending had been the most difficult part, as he struggled with the reality of his personal experience with the old man in the coffee shop and the need to create a fictional conclusion to the tale. But three months into the task, he managed a satisfactory ending and was happy to type those famous words "the end."

It was only then that Sam could tackle the last piece of his plan, which was what to do with his life. He intentionally held off on much reflection because he felt that writing the novel – and trying to get it published, of course – were critical inputs before he could make certain decisions. With those magic words added to the last page of the novel, he knew that plotting decisions on career would now be less painful. He was clear on what he wanted to do, and it wasn't advertising.

Sam pondered an appropriate celebration of the completion of his first novel, then shook his head. It wasn't time to celebrate. He had been such a recluse these past many weeks and yet his former social life did not beckon in the slightest. But he did note a strong belief that there would be more stories to come and for that he was indeed thankful.

Oddly enough, William Bell slithered into his mind, and for once, this thought was not immediately followed by feelings of guilt or rage. In a blink of an eye, he knew that he could now visit William, and that he subconsciously had been waiting until he completed the novel. That was the motivation he needed; out the door he went, his computer screen still showing those marvelous closing words.

15

William was sitting in a rocking chair on the porch, watching Sam's near-leap up the stairs. Funny, Sam thought; he'd never seen a soul on the porch before and yet it seemed a perfect place for a catch-up with William. William was his usual all-knowing self; by his chair was a bucket of iced beers. Sam had caringly brought a six-pack of Hoppy Endings to share.

William smiled, but said nothing. He slowly reached out with a bottle opener to open two of Sam's contribution, while Sam mentally confirmed that this indeed was the celebration he needed. No words were spoken as they clanked bottles and sipped their beer.

Finally, Sam began to speak. "Now I owe you an apology, William," he said contritely. "I get why you were so mad, and if it makes any difference, I took your counsel to heart." He explained in great detail all of his efforts over the past 12 weeks, the roller coaster of emotions throughout, and his cause for celebration – both the completion of draft one of his novel, as well as his decision to move forward with a career in writing. He even admitted his worries about getting the book published, as well as his willingness to try every avenue possible.

"Again, I owe you an apology and so much more," he concluded, with the last of his beer. "Me, myself and I have had a great deal of reflective time together lately, and it's because of you that I think I might be able to live the life I want."

William still said nothing, merely grabbing a second round

of beers and opening them. Taking a swig, he gazed at Sam with an expressionless face. Abruptly, he put down his beer.

"When I was a young fellow, I encountered some pretty significant teasing about my name," William began, sitting with elbows on knees, hands pressed together.

Sam leaned in. William rarely spoke about himself.

"Most kids get teased as youngsters, but the combination of my supposedly odd personality, and the last name of Bell encouraged many of my young peers. 'Ding, ding, ding,' they would chant, ad nauseum."

William's eyes brightened. "Of course, it caused me no embarrassment whatsoever. In fact, I challenged myself to find a positive definition of the term, though I was clearly aware that their intent wasn't as pure. I thought of it as a 'bell going off,' suggesting a new learning, an insight, an aha. As much as this sounds silly, I would say it to myself in class when I figured out some impossible problem. I would smirk at those fellows and they finally found it rather dull to try to insult me.

"So why do I share all this?"

Sam grinned and said "Yes, why ARE you sharing all this?"

William grinned back, then leaned as far forward as he could. "Ding, ding, ding, Sam Taylor. You, my friend, have had a sizeable insight, and I am so glad for you.

"I know a fabulous publisher," William eagerly continued. "When I wrote my book of poems, she was absolutely amazing to work with. I happened upon her at a creative yoga retreat long ago. I certainly can connect you with her."

Sam laughed to himself. Well, of course William had written a book of poems and of course he had participated in a creative yoga retreat. He would have to search for the book on Amazon.

117

"Well, thank you, William. I mean it. I have gained more than insight; I think epiphany might be the right word," Sam said. "I don't think I will be fighting you on this one."

William smiled his whimsical smile. "But you must indulge me. How did the spy adventure conclude? I must say I am quite curious to find out what happened."

Sam looked at him thoughtfully, took a hearty gulp of beer, and replied: "I guess you will have to read the novel, now won't you?"

SAM

One very relieved William here –

Well, that worked out quite well, don't you think? What an amazing transformation! Not only did Sam fall on his sword regarding his whining ways in my office following the receipt of my profound advice, he actually followed through and wrote that damn novel, not to mention a plan for his life! I still think "Rear Window" was a bit of a cheesy prop, but it worked; yes, it did. "Ding, ding, ding," indeed.

I also applaud myself for my fine acting when I pretended to be so angry at Sam. I didn't know I had it in me! I quickly realized I had to leverage his angst so that he could hear me. A nice learning for me as well.

Now, I must remember to thank my nephew who manages The Buzz. I told him that the fake fire was overdone, but he only looked at me and sarcastically said, "Who's overdoing it?" I can't imagine the insinuation. But his willingness to close for a day on my behalf – with appropriate compensation of course – not to mention the excellent ouster of Sam, were marks of an up and coming young man. It is so useful to have valued resources, now isn't it?

Yes, a fine caper indeed – that's just the word. Now it's time for another one.

—William

EMMA

Greetings once again.

Lastly, but certainly not least, (what awful English), please meet Emma, a small business attorney, who unfortunately deals with me when I am at my most frustrated. Yes, even I have moments of frustration, as perhaps you've noted, or perhaps not. For you see, I am a business person as well as a life facilitator, and I do want to get paid for services rendered – especially by my corporate clients. It seems a proper business protocol, all in all, though I do make occasional decisions in my facilitator role to offer my services "on the house" if you will. Fortunately, I have done well with my business over the years and can withstand the financial implications. And sometimes I simply can't help myself – the desire to help a fellow human achieve great things is greater than the need for remuneration.

However, occasionally a client may fail to pay, and I must confess I can get a bit testy about it. Even worse are those "irreconcilable differences" that can emerge in a business relationship. And that's when I count on an extraordinary resource: Emma.

She is capable of addressing a fairly broad variety of legal matters. As my attorney for many years, she has been kind enough to put up with my very strong and creative need for what might look like revenge on occasion and help me resolve matters in a calmer, more legal fashion. So now you know something about me as well as Emma. In fact, Emma also is a dear friend and you may see a side of me in this story that you haven't seen before.

While she manages to calm me down, never have I met such an intense person with such inspiring goals. Imagine: An attorney in metro Detroit who idly ponders the possibility of owning a horse farm. Now of course she doesn't know that I am aware of her deep desire for a horse farm. I just know. That's what I do.

She can be described in a plethora of words beginning with "P:" passionate, pushy, prickly, persuasive – my, the adjectives are pouring out. There are also "P" words that she is not: pretentious, passive, paranoid. But in a nutshell, my friends, she is a piece of work with a capital "P."

She works like a dog! No challenge is too sizeable for her to tackle. Her reputation for going for anything and everything is renowned. Yet, there's a part of Emma longing for something more in life, whether she currently knows it or not. When all is said and done, she'll be shaking her head in bewilderment, as you sometimes get what you ask for. Dear me – more bad grammar.

Ladies and gentlemen: Emma.

—William

1

High five; score one for the good guys. Emma Andrews rarely lost control of her emotions, at least in the courtroom, but in this case, a modest high-five was definitely in order. Her client's former wife was so sure that she had a case to keep those two kids who so deserved to stay with the father they love – who also clearly loved them. What a bitch! Running all over town with other men and leaving her kids alone at night. Then, when this poor sonuvabitch does the right thing and fights for custody, she tries to smear him with falsehoods. Fortunately, the judge saw right through the lies, and those kids get to go home with a parent – a parent in every sense of the word. It doesn't always turn out that way, Emma thought to herself, as her client sat back, wiping away a few tears as the shrew stalked out of the courtroom, ranting loudly at her attorneys. But it was moments like this that made her 24-7 job well worth it.

She headed out of the courtroom after happily conferring with her client on important next steps, with every intention of returning to the office for a few more hours of duking it out with client files. Emma paused at the top of the courthouse stairs and looked around. It was one of those beautiful afternoons in downtown Detroit, with the temperature in the 70s and a balmy breeze blowing off the beautiful Detroit River. Normally, Emma wouldn't even notice the weather, but after such a productive day in court, the breeze practically smacked her in the face. She felt one small cord of tension slip away and abruptly decided to call it a day.

125

That decision presented a problem, as it always did when she made such rash decisions: What should she do with a seemingly empty late afternoon and evening ahead of her?

William Bell immediately came to mind. Yes, she thought to herself; it's time to visit William. Her internal grin confirmed that the decision was the correct one, and she pointed her practical flat black shoes to the parking deck, thinking about this creative madcap who happened to be a dear client and friend.

As she headed north to nearby Birmingham in her Corvette convertible, she reflected on the day their paths first crossed some 15 years ago. She felt the hint of a smile as she remembered the day he blasted into the small law office where she was lucky to find a job after law school. Her smile widened, thinking of others' views of William as this calm, Zen-like man. Well that wasn't the case when his principles were violated; that was for sure. On that day long ago, he insisted in loud tones that he must speak to Edward – the firm's owner – immediately. There was only one problem: Edward was having the first vacation of his career in the Keys, having hired his first employee – Emma Andrews.

But she wasn't afraid of this tall, irritated man – not at all. After serving as a law clerk to a judge in Detroit's court system during law school, she was quite comfortable with a wide spectrum of humans. Emma calmly looked up from her small desk, squeezed into the corner of the second-floor office known as Edward Lake, Attorney-at-Law. "I am so sorry, sir, but Mr. Lake is out of town," she said professionally.

William's frustrated face lunged in her direction, seeming to conduct an instant x-ray of her inner organs. "And who are you?" he asked rather abruptly. "Did Edward hire an office manager at last?"

"He hired an attorney." She held out her hand. "Emma Andrews, attorney-at-law," she said, putting her newly-developed power handshake to work.

The touching of their hands, rather than the strength of Emma's grip, seemed to calm William down. His gaze returned to Emma's face, but shifted from anger to curiosity, as he began to leverage his innate ability to sense things about another human. For a moment, at least, William's energy and conversation shifted from whatever principle had been violated to a series of assumptions about her current lot in life: "You probably work long hours, don't you? And I suspect you don't take much time off. Yet you are still fairly early in your career …"

"Wait a gosh-darn moment!" Emma interrupted. William ceased the torrent of comments and looked somewhat surprised. "I sure don't need to be analyzed by a pissed-off passerby!" she continued, bristling a bit. "And I'll decide at some point what I want to share with you. Now, how can I help you?"

Emma now chuckled, thinking back to that first meeting with William, as she sailed along on the highway, driving precisely six miles over the speed limit. After her outburst, he shut up in a hurry and grew quite contemplative, she recalled. She actually was able to help him, once he shared his dilemma. It involved a person who insisted in parking in front of his office, even though William had gone to great lengths to secure a permanent parking place for himself. What was even more annoying to William was that the individual dumped his car's ashtray on the sidewalk each time he parked there. Emma and William partnered to creatively arrange for the city's parking enforcement officer to happen to wander by when the fellow tried to park there, and soon he chose to find another location for his parking and ashtray disposal needs.

Fifteen years passed quickly: Now Emma served as William's attorney of choice, and the firm of Edward Lake Attorney-at-Law had become Emma Andrews, Attorney-at-Law. The quick trip down memory lane, in the final few minutes of her trip, added to her positive mood as she fondly recalled many of their creative legal pursuits over the years. By the time she got to William's office, where his vehicle was of course parked in its normal spot, she was laughing aloud.

Emma briskly marched up the wooden steps to the top of the porch. Immediately, she could feel a modicum of release as she took in the Asian setting, the smell of lavender and the sound of perfectly-pitched chimes. The theme continued as she barreled in through the front door, not ever thinking about ringing the bell. Buddha stood in the foyer as if welcoming her personally. She patted him on the head, then swept straight down the hall to William's office. She could hear Debra, William's gifted and wonderful colleague, yell out a welcome and she hollered a hello in return. William's door was open, and she paused in the doorway, leaning against the doorway with her arms crossed, taking in the view.

If the outdoors could successfully thrive inside, particularly in Michigan with its fierce wintry season, it would be in this room. Emma always liked to spend a quick moment admiring the outrageously unique elements. Large boulders, planters filled with what appeared to be Michigan native plants, a stream running through the room, wind chimes burbling in the breeze. Dark rattan chairs in a sunny, warm corner of the room beckoned, where she could see William already waiting for her. It was one of his most frustrating yet wonderful qualities – the ability to know that she was coming to visit before she set foot in the place, even if she zipped in quietly. In fact, now that she thought of it, Debra seemed to have a similar gift. Interesting.

She made her way over to William, who was comfortably seated in one of the rattan chairs, with his fancy tea in front of him – and a hot cup of coffee, black – for her. He unfolded his ridiculously long legs and stood up, reaching for a hug. "Welcome. I am so glad you were able to come after your tedious trial. Congratulations on another win for the good guys."

She leaned in for the hug and smiled once again. Of course, he knew the outcome. If it wasn't his personal radar, it was his constant connection to every technological outlet known to mankind, or some peculiar combination of both. After years of denial, she had come to accept William's interesting attributes. She couldn't explain them, which annoyed her, but she certainly admired his outcomes.

She flopped down into the chair, grabbed the coffee and took a sip. Perfect dark roast, as always. "Thank you. I have to say that this one felt really good. That woman was a beeyatch. I wanted to scratch her eyes out!"

William smirked at Emma and sipped his tea. "I would guess that you experienced a tad of distaste regarding her mothering skills, right?" he said dryly.

"Don't get me started. It took every bit of my mental muscle not to get up and smack her across her perfectly made-up face as she smugly waited for the judgment. The joke was on her. Those little kids sure deserved better and they got it. My client is a great fellow who has been through the ringer. My heart really ached for him, and that made me want to take her down." Emma found herself getting angry all over again.

William leaned over and patted Emma's arm, thinking that he was certainly glad she was on his team. He didn't want to ponder the alternative. "So you headed this way."

"I made an abrupt decision to play hooky for the rest of the afternoon, then panicked," she replied lightly. "Suddenly, it seemed to make brilliant sense to visit you."

Emma thought about what she had just said. Why had she so rashly decided to invade William's space this afternoon? It was true that their business relationship had morphed into a true friendship as well. He knew more about her than practically anyone, but then he knew a lot about everyone. But she really wasn't quite sure why her compass pointed to William's office this day or what exactly what she hoped to accomplish, beyond not returning to her own office. Perhaps he needed some legal support. Perhaps she hadn't been fully present recently given the big trial …

William gazed at her in his typical intense way as he also started to form hypotheses for her visit to his office. She quickly started to shake her head. "Don't go there, William," she said.

"Go where?" he retorted calmly, head shifting to the side.

"You know where."

Emma took another sip of her coffee. He knew her too well, that was for sure.

William continued his reflection without her permission, hands folded with forefingers placed together, his favorite thinking pose. While some people would look absolutely idiotic in this pose, somehow it managed to work for him. "Maybe it is a sign that change is in the air," he continued. "Maybe working 20 hours a day is growing a tad much and your subconscious sent you the tiniest of messages. Maybe …"

"STOP!" Emma blurted out the admonition with such speed and precision that William dropped his hands, which fortunately were not holding his teacup. "I am thrilled with my work and my life, thank you very much. I don't know why I bothered to wander by."

She put down the cup, stood up and marched toward the window, in an effort to buy a couple of minutes to regain some sense of calm. She simply didn't understand what was wrong with her. As a state of calm proved elusive, she turned quickly back to William, just in time to take in a dry smile on his face. That seemed to infuriate her even more.

"You know, I remembered an important file that needs a look-see," she said in an artificial sing-song voice. "Bye now!"

With that she was out the door, down the hall and waving to Buddha, before William had a chance to utter a peep. Debra's faint "see you soon!" wafted through the porch window, but Emma was not close enough to hear it.

2

Emma did indeed return to her office, once the stuffy little second-floor space of dear Edward Lake. After working for Edward for several years, and growing to truly love the man, he abruptly announced his retirement one early June morning. "Emma, my dear, I'm done with it," he said heavily, stepping from foot to foot, as if nervous. "You must take over. You are an outstanding attorney."

She jumped up from her desk before he could exit the room, grabbing his arm. "Wait a minute, Edward! What in the world is going on? We have the Pittscott trial starting next week!"

"You will do fine my dear," Edward replied, uncharacteristically sounding curt. "I'll be heading out now."

She let him go, though her insides debated feelings of anxiety and relief. It seemed like yesterday that he marched down the stairs, only looking back at her once as he rounded the corner and disappeared from sight. Of course she soon learned that his wife Betty had used the ultimate threat to get her 74-year-old husband out of the law business: She was moving to Florida with or without him. It was a no-brainer; he would not have lasted a week without that wonderful woman. Emma managed the trial quite nicely, if she said so herself, and once Edward publicly announced that he was leaving the business, Betty graciously allowed him a transition period before their big move. Edward generously "sold" the business to Emma and paved the way perfectly with all of his clients. The transition was a piece of cake.

Before long, the downstairs space in the old building became available, and because Emma had put away almost every nickel she had ever earned, she was able to execute a major renovation, installing the office on the first floor, and a special living space on the second. It worked like a dream.

On this summer evening, while technically she returned to the office, her heart was not in it. After a casual review of the notes and files left by her assistant, she took the steps up to her private home.

No matter what was going on in her world, Emma was able to instantly reduce her stress level merely by walking in the second-floor doorway and taking in the view. She sighed contently, entering her version of a Montana farm house, if such a style officially exists, remembering fondly the many nights of Google searches for images that she could provide to her architect to convey her vision: the snippets of ranches, the random photos of unique plumbing arrangements and the many visuals of horses grazing in pastures, though it took awhile for the architect to understand the latter category.

The Googling paid off, as did the architect who deserved every buck he received. The original four rooms had been transformed into an open layout of rustic country elegance, with knotty pine walls and worn hickory floors, bold wooden arched ceilings and a fireplace made of field stone. An actual barn door separated her bedroom from the rest of the space. Over time, she had lovingly selected furniture and art depicting her view of an ideal life out West.

Emma was fiercely protective of her creation and went to considerable effort to meet colleagues and acquaintances elsewhere. Only William had visited her upstairs' quarters and that had only been for friendly competitive purposes when they were arguing about who had the better-engineered kitchen space. She was quite sure she had won that competition though he continued to disagree.

Her "farmhouse" served her well, helping her to unwind quickly each night and feel comfortable in her skin, at least for a few hours.

All she needed was a pasture and a stable of horses.

3

Emma changed into jeans and a fleece top and put her feet up, sipping on a cold beer. It was a new local brew, with lots of pizazz. She ruminated about the ups and downs of the day – the amazing sense of defeating evil in the form of that awful mother; the freeing feeling of taking off time from work, even for a short while; the awkwardness of her visit to see William and her sudden bolt from the premises. She shook her head and sipped her beer again.

Her cell phone rang, not surprisingly. She knew it was William before confirming it on the screen. The only question was whether to answer the call, but she quickly concluded that a call was better than a visit. She knocked back a gulp of beer then answered right before the call went to voicemail.

"William," she said as a greeting.

"Emma."

"I know why you are calling."

"I suppose you do."

She rubbed the side of her neck, imagining William at his desk in his wonderful office, legs elegantly crossed, looking mildly disturbed at his friend's behavior earlier that day. She knew she had to offer some explanation.

"I don't know," she offered somewhat tersely.

"You don't know what?" he asked.

She rolled her eyes. She hated when he tried to do his psycho-magic on her. Weren't there plenty of other people he could fix? she thought to herself.

Before she could make up something, William bailed her out. "I called to make sure you are alright. That wasn't the normal Emma who blasted out of here today."

"Yes, I am alright, William. I truly don't know what that was about, but I'm sipping a cold one and I promise to think about things."

"Okay then. Have a good evening." He ended the call.

Rubbing her neck yet again, to counter a dull ache, Emma sighed. She recalled one of the young children of the divorce case looking up at her while she tried to gently learn more about their wiring, and the child sweetly asking why she sighed so much. She hadn't even been aware of it, but it probably had something to do with her fierce reaction to this lovely child's mother, and what she was trying to do to her children. Emma had the unique opportunity to catch a glimpse of the mother yanking this very child down the courthouse hallway, spitting out pure poison, in contrast to the supposedly kind and caring mother that she made herself out to be in the courtroom.

Emma knew something about angry, vindictive mothers. Her mother had been an awful piece of work. Long gone from this earthly existence, mother dearest was one of those quintessential two-faced bitches who could play nice with all the grownups then make a daughter feel worthless. It made Emma seethe to recall that evil woman's nasty smile in the courtroom, so certain that she would get her way. She forced herself to mentally shut down the painful visual of both mothers and return to analyzing her abrupt behavior with William.

She didn't know why her short conversation with William had caused such a reaction. He had a valid point, and it certainly wasn't the first time he had shared it with her. But something was bugging her. It truly was not like her to take time off nor to run away. And all this sighing – it irritated her like hell to think that something was amiss.

She had a great life: Her home was amazing, her work was fulfilling, and she stayed nice and busy, just the way she liked it. Perhaps she didn't have a close cadre of buddies; all that interaction would certainly irritate her at some point. She never yearned for the night life; she was unimpressed with the social scene and quite content to simply relax after a long day of work. And romantic interests? Ha! Overrated. All she had to do was look at her client files to know that most of those wonderful romances ended up in divorce. Harsh? Yes, but true, she thought. Absolutely spot on.

She jumped off the couch and deposited the beer bottle into the recycling bin. Enough of this nonsense, she thought. She had some preparation to do for a new client meeting in the morning, and it was time to get at it. Nice and busy for sure. Case closed.

4

Emma leaned over her desk, elbows to the table, and propped up her chin in both hands. Oh Lordy, what a day: two new clients with financial troubles, another new client who was contemplating a separation from her husband due to infidelity, and massive paperwork to reach a decent solution in a bankruptcy. A fine day indeed – all 14 hours of it. "See William Bell? I don't work 20-hour days," she announced to the empty room, then laughed. Their conversation from a couple of weeks ago obviously still bugged her and it didn't help that their paths hadn't crossed since that afternoon.

She locked the door of the office, precisely at half past 8, noting that summer's evening light made it feel earlier. People were wandering the streets looking for things to do on this balmy night and she couldn't get upstairs to her haven fast enough. While she ate a fancy version of a TV dinner at her wooden roll top desk, she undertook one of her favorite past-times – a Google search of horse farm websites, both in the area and across the world. She loved the sense of peace from the horses in their pastures, the visual of a horse rolling on its back, the camaraderie and sense of herd among the horses. The people who appeared on the many websites clearly loved their horses; they seemed so in touch with nature, so content in life, she observed. Sighing, she clicked off Google and glanced at her calendar to prepare for the remainder of the week. The pace remained overwhelming and she knew she needed to call it a night soon. Still, she leaned back in her oversized leather chair and let in the tiniest of notions: What would it be like to spend time with horses? Would it be different this time?

The mental door slammed shut. Emma rose abruptly and began her evening routine of reviewing urgent emails from desperate clients, cramming more into her calendar for the week and rationalizing why she would work throughout the weekend. Then it was time for bed.

Sunday afternoon arrived in a hurry as she had worked a good portion of the weekend. Facing the start of a brand-new week, she allowed herself a brief moment of envy for those who utilized some – or all – of the weekend for personal and recreational purposes. She was well aware of her quick rationalization of the need to work the weekend, precluding any leisure time, a particularly consistent habit of hers. However, she found herself unexpectedly antsy, spurred on by a package she had received Saturday from none other than William. Apparently, he was worried about her. She picked up the sizeable stack of articles and read his note again, the feeling of antsiness shifting to irritation.

Emma – I found these lovely pieces on finding one's calling and thought of you. —William.

She sniffed in disdain as she looked at headlines from Oprah Magazine and Huffington Post – with a Harvard Business Review book summary as icing on the cake. And who in the hell sent hard copies of articles these days, though she knew full well that if William had sent them via email, she would have deleted them in an instant.

"What a bunch of hooey. What does he know about my calling?" she muttered to herself. "He is the client, not me. My calling has been crystal clear since I made the decision to enter law school: to be a damn fine attorney, to fight the fights, get people the help they need, to work like a dog, to do what's right. Damn you William!"

Emma fumed throughout her evening routine. Her calling drove her day in and day out. William had crossed a line this time and she had to do something about it.

Emma's night was tumultuous, and she woke up cranky, resenting the lack of sleep, the turning and tossing throughout the night. Her frustration with William shifted to outright anger, and she sent him a terse email upon arrival in her office downstairs.

"Knock it off. I cordially remind you that you are the client, not me. So leave it be!"

She later reflected that perhaps a couple of seconds more investment might have resulted in a slightly less chilly email, but it was a passing thought.

Not surprisingly, at slightly after 6 that evening, William ambled through the door of her office. Not surprisingly, she was on a long conference call with an agitated client regarding marital assets. She waved him off, and he took a chair in her small waiting area. Looking through the stack of magazines, he shook his head, thinking to himself that she really needed to up the quality of the magazine choices for her clients. Perhaps something like a *Wired* or *Fast Company,* rather than *Ladies Home Journal* and *Motor Trend. Oprah* would be a fine offering as would *Experience Life.* Of course, she did have a couple of worn copies of *Horse & Rider,* which was completely understandable to William, though he couldn't imagine many clients flicking through one as they waited to meet with Emma.

Without an interesting magazine for a diversion, William took in the sights. Emma's office digs were extremely different from her home digs, that was a certainty, he reflected. It was all business on this floor. The small waiting room looked more like one at a doctor's office, with its white walls, obligatory magazine rack and framed scenes of the countryside. There was nothing wrong with it, but it sent a signal of efficiency and no-nonsense, probably exactly what she wanted the room to portray. Her assistant Ethan worked at a tiny reception desk at the back of the waiting room, which probably suited him fine as the waiting room was usually empty. Of course, Ethan was long gone for the day. A small kitchenette backed up on the right side of the space, and her moderate-sized office opened on the left. She had windows out to the street, though the blinds were always down; a traditional green lawyer lamp on her credenza and a florescent light above provided adequate lighting. She kept her desk quite neat, but he knew for a fact that just out of sight were piles of documents, law books and notepads. Today, her desk was covered in legal debris, but by the end of the day, he knew it would be wiped clean, literally and figuratively, in preparation for the next day's battles.

As William's thoughts turned to Emma herself, she finished the call, stretched and looked out through her door at him, with no discernable expression whatsoever.

"Hello there!" he offered up as a start to the conversation. "I received your kindly-worded email and thought it might be useful to stroll down the street and check in."

The slightest of furrows appeared between her brows, William noticed. He could tell she was weighing her words. She clearly chose a slightly artificial tone.

"Top of the day to you, William!" she said brightly. "I'm hard at it here, as you can see."

William took a long look at the large clock behind the credenza, which now neared seven p.m. "Yes, I most certainly can. I am sure you must be close to done for the day; I can wait," he said echoing her tone.

Gritting her teeth, Emma smiled at him. William mimicked the teeth gritting perfectly and the intensity instantly went out of her sails. She leaned back, sighing heavily.

"There, now isn't that better?" he said, taking a seat in front of her desk.

"Okay, I know why you are here, William," she replied. "I apologize for the pissy little note. But good God, man, what a stack of crap! Reams of reading about finding one's calling? Really?"

"Okay, perhaps I overdid it a bit, but Emma, I'm worried about you," William said firmly. "No … don't interrupt. I want to say one really important thing. I know you. Something isn't quite right. I haven't gotten my head around it yet, but my radar is going off on your behalf. And you know more about that than the average person."

As if she pressed a button, a finely-designed set of armor emerged silently and effortlessly and arranged itself around her. She shuffled her papers with great fervor, allowing a folded newspaper to slide to the floor. William beat her to the punch and handed it to her. As William tried to continue, she placed her arms on her stack of papers and looked him straight in the eye. The tone of her icy voice was completely aligned with the contents of her response: "William you are so kind to worry on my behalf, but I am fine and dandy. Now, if you don't mind, I have another engagement. Can you let yourself out? Thank you."

Ironically, with apparently a little magic of her own, the phone began to ring. William had no other course but to depart.

5

It took three more hours of hard labor for Emma to calm down sufficiently to make the short trek up the stairs to her haven, though she would not find peace there this night. Fully aware of the need to sleep due to another crushing day to come, she paced her Montana farm house, trying not to stew about William's seemingly-single-minded focus. That was impossible, of course. Finally, she resorted to a rarely-used technique that she saved for emergency situations. She went into her hugely-capable kitchen, pulled out a brandy snifter and filled it to the brim with Bailey's and ice. She used this particular tonic for all sorts of emergencies, both good and bad, and it always seemed to assist with the situation. However, she was a practical person and deployed the strategy sparingly.

Returning to the living room, she curled up on her rich red couch, sipped her drink and looked around. How she loved this place. Sighing heavily, she used another familiar technique and searched her brain for the core issue causing her stress. It took a couple of sips for the searching to produce results, but out it came. She felt threatened. She put down her drink and folded her arms tightly to her chest. Threatened? What the hell is that about? What an odd word to pop out of nowhere, she thought to herself.

Emma got up from the couch and reluctantly made the difficult decision to cancel her early morning appointments. Clearly, this was going to be a two-Baileys night as she gave herself permission to go a little deeper. Sure enough, it was a long night of reflection.

Even with the last-minute calendar changes, the following day was rough. With her defenses down, Emma had to fight harder than usual with her fellow attorneys, impossible clients and unhelpful clerks in the court. She always knew that when everyone surrounding her acted like screeching idiots, it might not be them and she would grudgingly entertain the possibility that it just might be her. She also had her work cut out for her, trying to keep her messy thoughts at bay throughout the day. Fortunately, it was Friday, and for once, she was taking the whole weekend off, one of the actually productive insights that she had accomplished the night before.

One of her secrets, not that there were many people from whom to keep secrets, was her love of wandering the countryside, exploring horse farms. If her Montana farm abode was any clue, Emma loved horses, and had since childhood. Obviously, they had no part in her successful life as an adult on this planet, in the courtrooms of Detroit, but she sure enjoyed visiting horses on occasional weekends, IF she gave herself permission to do so. But after the brutal week and the self-torture she inflicted upon herself over William's comments, she deserved more than a Baileys or two – it was time to head to the horses.

Her approach was simple. She kept an eye out in the local paper for horse farms for sale. One would think this would be a rarity, but at least a handful would be on the market across the central part of Michigan at any given point in time, particularly during the beautiful summer days. While she obviously was not going to buy a horse farm, the owners didn't know that, and it was a perfect entrée to see a farm in action and, most importantly, spend time with horses. Further, it would give her the opportunity to frame her messy thoughts of the last few days in a much more pleasant setting.

Late Saturday morning found Emma heading to Holly, a beautiful area with rolling hills, pastures and lakes, and a cozy historical town, proudly boasting a supposedly haunted inn. It was only about 40 minutes away from her downtown Birmingham abode, yet it seemed another world when she arrived at Little River Farm. As she turned down the dirt road leading to the farm, she sighed a good sigh. On the left was a pasture with two horses, with the aforementioned little river flowing nearby. What appeared to be the main barn was directly behind the pasture. A second barn and more pastures surrounded it. Up the hill were even more horses, and what appeared to be a home. She checked the sign at the gate – yep, this place was for sale. From her first glimpse, she couldn't imagine anyone wanting to sell it.

A young man came out of the main barn and waved. She drove up to him, and parked across from the stable doors. "Hey there," he said cheerfully. "How can I help you?"

"I'm exploring farms for sale around the area," she said. "I saw the ad for this one and thought I'd wander by. My name is Emma, Emma Andrews, by the way."

"Joe Johnson," the man said, reaching out a hand. "I manage the stables here. We are getting a fair amount of traffic right now, with the sign up. I just got off the phone with a fellow arranging a visit for tomorrow. Can I give you a tour or would you rather take a look on your own?"

A funny prickly feeling came over her as she digested the fact that someone else was planning to tour the farm, an oddly possessive feeling and clearly illogical. "I don't need to bother you," she replied. "I would be pleased to explore on my own, if that's okay with you."

"Absolutely!" Joe said. "These horses need lunch anyway. Let me know if I can answer any questions."

He headed back into the barn, and Emma was left to her own pursuits. She didn't move one muscle, preferring to slowly take in the sights, sounds and smells around her: Horses grazing in pastures, their tails swishing. Barn swallows dive-bombing the fields, then returning to nests snuggled under the rafters of the barn. Families of geese bathing in the pond between the two barns. The smell of hay. A breeze to grab and take with you. She relaxed and experienced an unusual moment of pure contentment; it was the best she had felt in many days.

She walked toward the other barn and took a peek inside. Kittens scattered into a stall filled with bales of hay, but the rest of the stalls were empty, as the horses were certainly out in the pastures for the day. Heading back outside, she was drawn to a pasture behind the barn, where a few horses stood in a herd munching on hay. As she neared, one horse looked up and checked her out. She was delighted and leaned over the fence, hoping the horse would come over to visit. As often is the case, the horse trotted over to say hello. He was a beauty, Emma thought, feeling the warm breath of the horse on her fist, which is how horses say hello. He was a little shy, but stayed right with Emma, and after a few minutes of getting to know one another, allowed her to pat his neck.

The stunning black Arabian soon slowly wandered back to the hay feeder for the rest of his lunch. It was only then that Emma allowed her mind to reflect on the events of the past week, and particularly, the painful word "threatened." Out here on the farm, the word didn't sound so awful. She had tortured herself thoroughly on Baileys night, thinking of her past and creating a hypothesis of why she might feel threatened. Perhaps it was too strong a word, she rationalized, though her reaction to William's comments certainly would suggest she had felt some extreme feelings of the negative variety.

Emma knew herself well. She understood quite clearly what caused her enormous drive to work like a dog and to follow the rules that she had put in place for success. Childhood had been a tough venture for her. Raised by the previously mentioned two-faced bitch and a father who had gone through his own learning curve, resulting in deference to his controlling wife, Emma struggled mightily to thrive. Fortunately and unfortunately, young Emma was nothing like either of her parents. She had been a tree-climbing tomboy as a child, always ready for adventure. This was simply not in keeping with the young lady her mother was trying to create; she cringed at Emma's presence most days, forcing her to change into fussy clothing and adhere to her twisted view of appropriate social standards in their small southwestern Michigan town. Father ran the bank and stayed out of his wife's way. Mother anointed herself matriarch of the village and tried to control everything. While most of the town's "high society" folks toed the line, Emma had a hard time doing so. She regularly faced painful consequences as a result, from vicious lectures to being grounded for days, and even a lashing on many occasions. Indeed, her mother's creativity in finding unique ways to punish her daughter probably deserved some sort of award for outstanding evil, Emma thought bitterly, not allowing her mind to go too far down a very dark and twisted memory lane.

As she grew up, Emma had plenty of time to figure out that she wanted absolutely nothing to do with her parents and their lifestyle. She forced herself to cease the outside adventures and daydreaming and to focus on her schoolwork. While getting a job certainly wasn't expected of her, Emma used her growing negotiating skills to persuade her parents that working at the bank would provide her important relationship-building skills. She graduated at the top of her class in high school and, once again, was able to get her mother to believe that a college education was absolutely required to assure the finest possible marriage. Ha! Emma thought to herself. That was a good one.

From that point on, things started to get better. While her parents paid for her schooling, reminding her constantly of their many sacrifices on her behalf, she quietly worked two jobs and studied like a crazy person, putting all possible income away for law school. She was too busy to have any interaction with her parents whatsoever, and Mrs. Bitch was too busy running the town and her husband to bother with a daughter she never cared for anyway. Scholarships, savings and loans combined to pay for law school, serving as crucial testimony on why she didn't need to come home and enter into a loveless marriage with some society dude, infuriating her mother. Off she went, never looking back, and systematically shedding – or burying – her memories of a very painful childhood.

Yet on occasion, her mother still seemed to have the power to wander into her brain to whip her into shape. Emma worked hard to deny her access, and that was through being a hard-working, successful attorney. She would never steer off-course. No wonder she felt threatened by William's laser-like focus on her well-being.

A loud snort caused Emma to look up in surprise. The horse had returned to the fence and it was almost as if he could read her thoughts and didn't agree with them. Emma grinned at the horse, reaching out to pat him once again. But the horse snorted and turned his back.

"That's Raven," said a deep raspy voice next to her. Emma jumped, then automatically stiffened at the name. Another Raven? The thought flitted through her brain as she observed that she had been so in the moment with the horse that she hadn't noticed anyone walking up to her. "He's a little skittish, but I think he was talking to you right then."

"I had the same thought!" Emma replied, compressing her thoughts and turning to the old fellow who stood by her side. "I'm Emma Andrews, here to see this beautiful farm."

"I'm Bruce Rivers. Joe told me we had someone checking out the place. I'm owner and would be glad to answer any questions you have."

Emma felt a slight twinge of guilt but found the gumption to look directly in his eyes and shake his hand. He was up there in years, with the look that many owners of horse farms have – weathered face, tan arms, the requisite old blue jeans. He wore a baseball cap rather than a cowboy hat, in honor of the Detroit Tigers. His cowboy boots showed memories of many days managing the farm.

"I do have a question," Emma said, surprising herself. "Why in the world are you selling this wonderful place?"

Bruce leaned on the fence and looked out at the horses. "I've said this a bunch of times, and it never feels good to say it, but I'm gettin' old. My kids are all busy hotshots in Chicago and New York. They don't want to run a farm. They act like they're allergic to horse poop, for God's sake. Joe is a great help, but he can't afford to buy it. And his skills are managing the horses, not dealing with all the finances, supplies and other stuff required to run a farm. My kids are on me to move closer to them, not that I want to. You know, all those later-in-life sorta things coming at me all at once."

Emma felt genuine sorrow for the old fellow. "I'm sorry," she said softly. "That must be really tough."

"Aw, it will be okay," he said roughly, then softened as he looked her over. "Now tell me why you want to buy a horse farm, though I already can tell you have a special relationship with horses."

Quickly, Emma retreated. "Oh, I am just looking around. It's a pipe dream, really, but I get lured out to look at various properties now and again. But I need to get going now; I realize that I have an appointment shortly. It was very nice to meet you and I wish you the best. Seriously. I mean it."

"Well come back and visit again," Bruce replied. He smiled at her, tipped his baseball hat, and ambled off.

Again, the black horse snorted, then pawed the ground and headed to the far side of the pasture, seeming to call her out on her lack of candor. On that note, Emma headed home. For she did have someplace to be – she needed to think about a horse named Raven: the same name of a horse from her childhood, one of those memories that had been locked safely away. Then she probably needed to figure out how to get William off her back.

6

William spent his Saturday morning in deep reflection. While this was not an unusual exercise, even Debra was surprised at his intensity, particularly after he strongly suggested that she depart for the remainder of the day. Her work schedule was as eclectic as William himself. So it wasn't unusual for her to spend a few hours of a Saturday catching up with William's ever-crazy list of assignments to support his fascinating work.

"Are you sure you are okay," Debra asked. "You seem a little aggressive today."

William peered at one of his favorite people and hissed. "I'm fine, Debra. Just let me be."

She threw up her arms in resignation, packed up her stuff and ambled down the front porch steps. She knew he was about to undertake a marathon of some sort, and she was going to find her friend Cate and persuade her to have lunch.

William sought the peace of his beloved office and began a ritual that had served him well over the years. As he circled the room repeatedly at a solid pace, he tried to get after the essence of the issue that was Emma. Talking aloud, William explored his gut's strong conviction that something was off kilter with her supposed passion and purpose in life. Yes, he had known Emma for years and years, and she always worked tirelessly; she was too busy to have a social life. He knew her parents were deceased though she never talked about either of them in any detail; the mere mention of them causing icicles to form in her eyes. He paused in his pacing to acknowledge how truly little he knew about Emma's background. Clearly, she liked farms and horses, but to his knowledge, she didn't incorporate any of this into her life, beyond her brilliantly decorated home space. Too busy, she would say if asked about any other possible activity beyond her work.

Commencing the pacing again, William thought about his own situation, and how absolutely critical both purpose and passion had always been. Was he so different from Emma? Why yes, he was. He had a gift and had been lucky enough to craft a career and life that honored it. He would cheerfully avoid any work or relationships that didn't align with his sense of purpose or caused his radar to shudder in horror. But Emma … yes, she could be feisty and upbeat, but she did anything and everything asked of her by anyone and everybody. William finally pulled out from deep within what he had been fussing about for so long: A sizeable conflict pulsated in his dear friend Emma, and it was getting worse over time. No wonder she seemed to look almost threatened when they last met. Armed with that new insight, he changed the direction of the pacing, upped his speed and carried on.

A couple of hours later, he sank into his rocking chair, rocking steadily as he thought about the clues he had gathered from recent interactions: two magazines in her waiting room, a folded newspaper that had fallen on the floor in her office and Emma's look of almost panic as she covered the offending newspaper and abruptly sent him on his way. Then there was the extensive anger she oozed when talking about the courtroom scene involving the divorcing mother. It was all he needed to concoct a hypothesis and weave a fine strategy that might help get to the bottom of things. After making a quick call, he still had time to put together a little scenario and present it to Emma before the day was done. Eyes twinkling, William realized that he was doing exactly what he loved to do best. He hoped that his little intervention would allow Emma to do the same.

Emma returned in the late afternoon and found William camped outside of her office, lanky leg leaning against the brick wall, tea in hand. She smirked a bit as she watched him fidget; he looked like a little kid – no, a great big kid – waiting to get in on a game of some sort.

He straightened up quickly when he saw her, raising his cup to her as in celebration. He sure looked alert, she thought, then as she contemplated the implications of that, frowned slightly at him. This didn't bode well.

He not only saw the frown but could almost feel her brain working in overtime. He decided to start with the frown.

"Are you still mad?" he asked, as she reached him at her door. "I hope not, because I come bearing gifts."

A distinct sense of unease swirled around Emma. She unlocked the door, then signaled him in, struggling briefly with whether to see him in the office, or take him upstairs. The comfort of home won the battle, and up the stairs they went.

"No, I am not mad, though I am suspicious," she replied belatedly. "You seem a little off the wall for some reason."

Confirming that he was all set with his tea, Emma grabbed a glass of water and joined him in the living area. Again, she noted an excess of exuberance from the man, who already was known for being quite high energy. What could have him so geeked up? she wondered, and her lawyer-grown intuition set off a low peal of warning.

William jumped right in. "First. I do want to apologize. Again. I've given the matter serious consideration and I failed to communicate effectively with you, after knowing you all these years. You are a woman of action, and I was much too passive in my approach."

Emma stared at him. This was not sounding good at all. She knew William, knew how well he anticipated and communicated. What was going on? She knew without a shadow of a doubt that she was going to find out and that she wasn't going to enjoy it.

"With that said, I want to tell you of an action I took today. I need your help. Then I can get back to being the annoying client and you can provide your sterling counsel. Sound good?"

She grudgingly leaned forward, not trusting his motives one iota.

"Okay then!" William said cheerfully, standing up as if he was about to make a major announcement. "Today, I decided to buy a farm near Holly. I found it for sale on the Internet and have arranged to tour it tomorrow. Now before you get all lawyer-like and tell me that I simply can't do that, I have to tell you that my radar really went crazy about this farm. Coincidentally, Debra knows the owner, and his kids are insisting that he needs to move closer to them. That's why he's selling. I need a new project and I really believe that I can convert the farm into a profitable agricultural business. Apparently, the land is fertile beyond measure, just wasting away while horses prance about doing whatever it is that horses do. I imagine soybeans. Perhaps there's even the possibility of new crops – perhaps this can be part of the urban agriculture movement here in Metro Detroit. I have to say it's the type of new adventure I like to seek out."

William intentionally avoided looking at Emma, though he

154

mentally patted himself on the back for the brilliant addition of soybeans to the conversation.

Emma's head began to throb as William sat down, sipped his tea and blathered on about new-age vegetables. She couldn't believe how incredibly hurt and furious she felt at this moment in time, even while recognizing that William knew absolutely nothing about her secret weekend pursuits at horse farms. She found herself without a single idea on how to handle the situation. Worse, she didn't have a chance in hell of pulling off an air of neutrality.

As her brain faced that reality, she managed to observe that William was now staring at her with his classic concerned expression, causing the fire within her to grow exponentially. Yet instead of exploding in rage, she unexpectedly burst into tears. They were not pretty tears. Some women can cry delicately and then appear as if nothing had ever marred their faces. That was not the case with Emma; if she was going to get upset enough to cry, which rarely occurred, it was going to be a crying marathon. This was no exception.

William appeared uncharacteristically awkward. He sank into the chair beside her and tried to hold her hand to no avail. He strode to the kitchen to take stock of possible adult beverages that could be useful. He handed over tissues. After being waved off several times, he finally sat across from her, his acutely-angled knees jiggling.

After a long 20 minutes, Emma's sobs subsided. As is usually the case, the damage to her face had been done. Her eyes peered through puffy slits. Her cheeks looked raw and what looked like little bruises began to pop up under her eyes.

She silently held out her hand for the beverage William had selected, a cold oaky Chardonnay. He also offered more tissue and she took that as well. She settled back in her chair, sniffed, and started to speak.

"The horse was named Raven. My parents bought him because the so-called 'upper class' members of the community owned horses. Oh, how I loved that horse. My mother hated Raven, and Raven hated her. Worse still, my mother absolutely loathed the relationship that Raven and I had together."

Emma's tears dried as her blood pressure increased. "But that was all par for the course. Because my mother hated me, and I hated my mother. It was no surprise that my father stayed at the bank for every moment he could to escape the evil witch's controlling ways. I was not so lucky."

Emma chuckled in a somewhat evil-sounding way.

"Believe it or not, William, I was a wild sprite of a child. I loved our house in the country; I loved to sit in the top of our apple tree and ponder the world. I would sit behind our very expensive albeit empty barn and listen to the drone of the airplane above, thinking about what my life would bring. Until Mother would screech for me to come in and welcome the latest batch of her adoring fan club to a tea or a cocktail party.

"I would make my way into the house and she would grab me by the arm and whip it behind my back, muttering about how I was the worst thing that had ever happened to her. I was to get my clothes changed immediately and come out smiling like an angel. Really, that's what she would say, along with reminding me that I was an awful, dirty child, and that I was going to be punished in ways I couldn't imagine. I would emerge dressed like that angel, always desperately hoping to avoid some of her more creative punishments. I won't go there, but she was a master at coming up with novel ideas in that regard. And she would smile like an angel, sweetly asking me to bring them more crumpets or something of the sort."

She sipped the wine again, blew her nose like a trumpet, and continued.

"Then Raven appeared. Talk about a mixed message! This little kid couldn't get her arms around the fact that my parents would have bought a horse – bought me a horse! Obviously, she couldn't share the real reason – her need to keep up with the Joneses – so, at first, she reluctantly went along with the idea that it was good for my development as a young lady. It sure worked for me. Raven and I bonded fast and furiously, and the more we bonded, the more pissed off dear Mommy became."

William could feel Emma's emotions escalating but uttered not a word.

"I'm sure you can figure out what happened. One day, I came home from school, and Raven wasn't in his pasture. I looked in that perfect barn and no Raven. I started to panic, thinking that maybe I had left the gate open or something. Then I saw Mother, dressed in her going to town dress and heels, breezily making her way toward me. 'What's wrong, darling? Missing something?' Her eyes offered up this crazy combination of joy and revenge. Before I could utter a word, she continued: 'He's gone, darling. And you won't find him. Ever.'"

William gasped. But he didn't move.

"I threw up, to my mother's horror and thrill. Needless to say, this was the ultimate in evil parental behavior. My father never said a word about it. My mother grinned maniacally for days. I felt broken beyond measure and in the coming weeks and months, during many groundings for perceived insults and misbehavior, I grew up and decided that I needed to get away from these people. I won't bore you with all the details, but I became a very different person and I got out of Dodge. I crushed high school, college and law school. I know how to work hard, very hard. I buttoned up and buttoned up good; it's how I coped – how I cope even now. And it took some darn good coping when I was dealing with that awful mother in the divorce proceedings, let me tell you.

"But somewhere along the way, the better memories of Raven trotted back into my life in a good way – thus the western theme here, as well as an occasional visit to a horse farm. Yes, I like to visit horse farms. I even explored the concept of finding Raven but couldn't put myself through the torture of the exercise."

Emma put down the glass of wine and stood up, looking William straight in the eye.

"Guess what? I was at a horse farm in Holly today, William. I met a wonderful horse. It's the best I've felt in weeks. Now you show up with this news."

Emma's eyes glittered. William leaned forward to interject.

"No. Don't say a word. I want you to get the hell out of my place!"

She headed to the door, and gestured William out, more tears rolling down her face.

As William beat a hasty exit, Emma knocked back her wine and immediately threw up.

7

Emma disappeared. She flat out disappeared, and William was unable to find neither hide nor hair of her, though he didn't try very hard to sense where she might be. The pimply simpleton who worked for Emma tentatively informed William that Emma was "away" when he came to her office on Monday morning.

"Define 'away,'" William commanded tersely.

That was all the young fellow could muster; he babbled the word several times, then fled to the bathroom.

William took advantage of the opportunity to take the stairs three at a time and bang on Emma's door. He didn't expect an answer and didn't get one. He scratched his chin thoughtfully as he mulled over the possibilities. He certainly wasn't surprised to find her gone; the amount of abuse dear Emma had endured was frightening to say the least. But the key question in his inquisitive mind was whether she would do something foolhardy in her incredibly vulnerable current state.

William had known Emma for a very long time and he knew full well that she kept a great deal of herself hidden behind a very crusty exterior. Yet even he was surprised at the depth of the emotional and physical abuse she had neatly packaged and put away. While William was a supporter of "letting it all out," he knew that opening Pandora's mental box could be highly dangerous. Frankly, he concluded, he was worried. With that conclusion drawn, William knew he had to find Emma and find her fast.

While he had some idea of where to look, William headed back to his office to seek the one person who he trusted to offer some insightful commentary: Debra. Wasting no time, he spilled the entire sordid story. He intuitively knew that she would have a nugget of contribution to offer, and she most certainly did.

"If it were me, I'd head to the horse farm," Debra said solemnly, wiping a tear on behalf of Emma's painful past. "Some might not have the courage to take such a bold step, but Emma would. You need to be careful here, William. She is going to be like a wild horse; she will bolt and hurt you if you aren't careful. And she could end up hurting herself even more."

Debra sent a strong message of support to William, thinking of her own journey and his incredible sensitivity and care for practically a stranger. She smiled. "I know you will be your normal intuitive self. Go after her. I'll be sending major energy out into the universe on her behalf."

William's eyes crinkled briefly at the corners before he headed straight back to his office to continue crafting "Operation Keep Emma Safe and Help Her Achieve Her Dreams." It was a lengthy title, but he wasn't going to take the time to edit it when there were more pressing matters to consider, particularly how tough it would be to avoid crushing the spirit of a wild mustang of a human. It would take some doing but he happened to have another interesting idea.

8

A very fragile Emma sat on a huge boulder in a field full of mares, holding on to her knees for dear life. The mares stared at her from afar, all gathered up in a tight herd. She could only imagine what vibes they were getting from her right now. It had been a daring move, coming to the farm, explaining at least part of her situation to Joe, so that she could gain permission to wander in the pastures and be with the horses again. He couldn't have been more accommodating, probably picking up her mood as easily as the horses were now doing.

"Make sure you find the big rock in the mare pasture," he advised kindly, pointing up the hill. "It's a good place to sit and think."

She thanked him profusely, quickly deciding not to analyze the counsel, but to head straight to the rock. So here she was, on a beautiful sunny breezy day, on top of a hill, with the whole farm stretching out in front of her. Now if she could only stop holding herself so tight. But that wasn't going to happen for a while.

Emma attempted a deep breath, knowing that she needed to calm down in order to think things through. While focused on the gargantuan task of breathing, she failed to notice a line of horses heading her way. She looked up to find herself literally surrounded by horses – at least 10 of them by her quick count. Amazingly, she wasn't unnerved in the slightest. Her incredible sickness of spirit over her beloved Raven stayed at bay as she slowly held out her softly-closed fist to say hello.

Each horse seemed to take a turn connecting with Emma, some even gently caressing her arms with their soft lips. She could literally feel her spirit settle down thanks to the intuitive ministering of this wonderful herd of horses. She was able to finally take that deep breath and her herd breathed right with her.

A couple of hours later, Emma headed to the next place she knew she had to visit: the pasture of Raven – the beautiful black Arabian who had communicated so deeply with her during her first visit to the farm. She knew it was going to take every smidgeon of her courage to go visit that horse. Then there was the matter of William. She was smart enough to know that he would be seeking her out quickly. She tried to hold on to the calming influence of the mares and keep William out of her head. She would have to deal with him later – much later.

Within minutes, she was at the gate of Raven's pasture. He was calmly eating hay, though his ears stood straight up as she approached. She leaned against the gate, gripping the bar, trying to breathe deeply. The horse backed away and headed to the corner of the pasture, probably disturbed by so much negative energy. While Emma logically understood that reality, she couldn't avoid the incredible pain and guilt she held in her heart for the original Raven, the not knowing of what happened to that dear, sweet horse of her childhood. She leaned her head on the gate and sobbed.

9

William found himself in a country study in the main house at the farm, drinking a cold one with none other than Bruce Rivers, the farm's owner, a fine man with deep compassion. William had completed a carefully condensed overview of Emma's situation and was pleased to see the older man's eyes glistening with a couple of tears on her behalf. This may work out, he thought to himself.

"That's almost criminal," Bruce said, shaking his head. "Simply criminal. The damage humans do to so many ... it makes my heart ache to think about it! And that poor girl ..."

He paused for a minute, holding his head in his hand, then taking a long swig of his beer. "You know, I sensed something wild and broken in her when I met her," he said, looking straight at William. "Don't get me wrong; she was confident and strong. But there was something about her, and damned if Raven didn't pick up on it right away. And the fact that she had her own Raven from childhood taken away from her so brutally. Her mother must have been a beast of a woman."

"Raven? You mean there's a Raven here on the farm?" William found himself surprisingly flustered by this news, a rare situation indeed.

"Why sure!" Bruce replied. "Raven is a great big Arabian; Emma spent some time with him when she visited, and he told her a few things about life. Horses are amazing coaches to us humans, you know."

William's mind swept into action as Bruce continued to talk

about the many gifts that horses have. Once again, he found himself with a brilliant solution to a delicate problem with a very strong woman, and he knew exactly how to address it.

"Bruce, I wonder if you and I can explore a special arrangement," William began, leaning back and sipping his beer.

10

The last of the gut-busting sobs ceased, leaving Emma feeling a wreck. Well, it was better than non-stop vomiting, she thought to herself wryly, as she lifted her head to survey the pasture. A small smile tinkered with her face as she took in the sight of Raven, standing a few short steps away. She was amazed that he wasn't fazed by such an onslaught; it clearly takes a strong horse to not bolt when dealing with such stuff.

Raven stepped forward, gently blowing on her outstretched fist. Emma struggled not to cry, yet again, as his huge head came toward hers and he breathed on her tears. A gentle snort led her to imagine that he was speaking for a Raven from the past, suggesting that she could let go some of the angst that she had held on to for so many years. She could feel all sorts of fresh feelings flood into the space she had locked up for so long: relief, curiosity, perhaps even something resembling the beginnings of peace.

Raven didn't move from her side when she heard footsteps come up from behind her. "Hi ya, Emma," said the gruff voice from her first visit to the farm.

She slowly turned her head, reluctant to move one inch from her new-found companion and ally. There was Bruce, who had been so open with his story when they first met. "Are you okay there honey?" he asked. "Though it appears Raven's got you well taken care of there."

"Hi ya, Bruce," she said hoarsely, as if she hadn't spoken in a very long time. Trying to find a bit of a smile, she added, "yes, I'm being very well taken care of."

They all stood together quietly for a few moments after Raven said "hello" to Bruce. Finally, Bruce took off his hat and turned to Emma. "Honey – I hope it's okay if I call you that. I need to talk to you about the farm. I sense that this may not be the right time for such talk but it's important that I share this with you."

Raven grunted slightly and continued to stand close to Emma.

"It's okay, Bruce," she replied. "I know the farm is going to be sold, and I'm coming to grips with that – along with a whole bunch of other things."

"Well, about that," he said. "There's been a development. Your attorney came here today and successfully negotiated the sale of the farm on your behalf. I did have another offer pending, but this one was a better one for a whole helluva lot of reasons."

Raven's tail swished mightily while Emma stared blankly at Bruce. "My attorney?" she said, trying to get her arms around such a thought. "I don't have an attorney. And I have it on good authority that this place is sold."

"Well, all I can say is that you need to come over to the house. Your attorney says he's ready to prepare all the paperwork after the three of us have a little talk. And I am sure ready to sign on the dotted line after talking things through with him. Damn fine fellow if I say so myself."

Emma didn't feel strong enough for her legal brain to come to attention and tackle this latest thorny chapter. Raven pawed the ground, still not moving away from the gate. William. It must be William, she thought. This is nonsense. I can't buy a horse farm! But she found she was between a rock and a hard place – Bruce and the beautiful Raven, who clearly supported the proposition. There was even a chorus of whinnies from the mares on the hill, adding their votes of yes. Before she could grab her all-too-familiar cloak of anger and vamoose, Bruce held his arm out and said "Come on. Let's go talk this out. It's gonna be okay."

Raven nickered his approval, and finally turned around, seeking a particularly green patch of grass. Emma found herself letting go of the gate and heading to the house with Bruce, knowing full well that the wily and wonderful William awaited them inside, and allowing in a slight sense of positivity about what was about to come.

11

"So how did you know I wouldn't bolt? That I wouldn't flat out turn down the opportunity to buy the farm?"

Emma and William sat on the boulder in the mares' pasture, watching the herd graze. A couple of days had zipped by since she signed on many a dotted line and found herself an amazingly-thrilled owner of a horse farm. It was done without a lot of fanfare, and Emma had barely looked at the documents. She easily picked up a pen and scribbled her signature. Her lawyer self shrieked at the lack of thorough review, yet she acknowledged that some significant changes were going on inside of her – and around her.

"I didn't know," William replied. "This whole situation required some serious reflection, since I am the party guilty of opening the barn door, excuse the pun. I was able to find a few clues that helped me develop a plan of action. Frankly, I wasn't quite sure what I was going to do when I arrived, which was highly unusual for me. But after talking with Bruce and finding out about your new best friend Raven, I had a hunch that you might be willing to do what you really wanted to do – which was to buy this farm.

"But I quickly concluded that I wasn't the one to persuade you. You were not exactly thrilled with me at that point in time." William smiled wryly. "I had to send the right negotiating party out to you. I have to say it was a bit difficult sitting in that house, hoping that all would go well. Yes, I know that

I was uncharacteristically nervous about all this, but you are a little different from my average client."

Emma nodded, guessing that he exaggerated slightly, imagining him stalking the halls of the farmhouse and peering out of the window to try to get a glimpse of what was happening. She knew he liked to be leading the parade with these types of "propositions."

"I'm no horse person," William continued, "but my gut was pretty vocal that you needed to own this farm. You needed Raven, as Raven needs you. No soybeans involved, I promise."

Emma stared down at Raven in the nearby pasture, as he lifted his head and appeared to look directly at her. She could feel his support in her heart. In fact, her heart was feeling pretty darn good at the moment, though she still felt a bit weak from the dramatic pace of events from the last few weeks. And now she had a very important message for her friend William.

"William. Hear me all the way through on this because I am about to try on the new me and say something kind of mushy right now. Thank you. And I mean it! Your methods are outrageous sometimes, but your heart is as big as that barn over there. I have to say that I was desperately trying to hold on to my sassy work-hard-leave-me-alone persona, and you wouldn't let that happen. I simply can't thank you enough. I think I am going to be one happy horse farm owner."

He bowed his head and tried to look humble, but of course it didn't work. "Well I certainly needed to make sure that my favorite attorney retains her sass but lives her dreams," he replied with a sparkle in his eye. "And I do need to talk to you about a small legal situation I'm enduring ..."

Emma burst into laughter. "No worries, William. I will still be around to save you from yourself. But don't be surprised if you have to come to my new satellite office here at the farm. I have some horses to tend to."

She laughed again as a certain horse threw in his own two cents via a loud whinny from the pasture below.

A CONCLUDING WORD (OR TWO) ...

There you have it: three lives, a little gentle facilitation and a few adventures along the way. I suspect you wouldn't mind a little update on these dear people.

Let me first dispel any readers with rose-colored glasses who hoped that any or all of these individuals would end up paired up, as if this was some traditional romantic novel. May I allow myself a "hrrumpphhh." Life isn't like that, even if executed through the capable hands of a life facilitator – Oh I hate that term. Note to self: Find a new title for my work.

Debra remains my office manager though we have changed her title to "vice president of transformation." There are plenty of opportunities for her to leverage her amazing skills to transform all sorts of things – including me. And it is amazing to see how she's blossomed as a human.

Sam published his book; no surprise to me, the publisher snapped it up in a hurry and that doesn't happen in the publishing industry these days. It appears elderly spies in coffee shops are hot in the literary world. He is now haunting historical bars, hoping for fodder for a second book.

Emma has reconstructed her entire life. She hired a young attorney to take on a good portion of her work, allowing her to spend more time at her new farm. I won't be surprised a tad if she abruptly decides to hand the practice over to this new hire and devote herself to the horses. Emma persuaded Joe to continue in his role and encouraged Bruce to visit as often as he wishes, a set-up that works well for all.

I suspect you might appreciate an update from me. I continue to search out fascinating people and problems, in the hopes that I might be of assistance. How I love this work! I am exploring a particularly interesting caper right now, but that's a story for another day …

On to the next adventure! All my best on your adventures too.

—William

A FEW MORE CONCLUDING WORDS

How to craft any conclusions about William Bell? Is he for real? What motivates him? And how does he do these crazy things?

We suspect you wonderful readers are asking these very questions. We have a question as well: How does one deal with a person like William? That could be a variation of a famous song "How do you solve a problem like Maria?" How does William manage to piss off people so easily? How does his famous intuition actually work? Or is it more than intuition? How can someone so snarky be so nice? Our questions go on and on.

Our gift to you for reading our stories is a little more information about William Bell. Here goes: William is the real deal and he truly hates the title of "life facilitator," which he certainly makes clear to anyone and everyone. If he could find a title that fits, he would take it in a second.

He is his own unique brand of human – perhaps we could gently joke that he takes "human" to a new level. Without bolstering his ego, which certainly would not be a good thing, William is a brilliant eccentric with a caring soul. As to his motivations, he has an unusual ability to fall into just the kind of projects that give him the most joy. Frankly, it's uncanny. His intentions are truly pure and positive, though his approach can be a little intense – creative, but consuming. We are convinced that the world could benefit with a few Williams around, not that we are aware of any others!

We are hopeful that William will share more stories in the future with regard to his fascinating adventures helping people. And perhaps, in doing so, we all will get more answers to our questions!

All the best from us as well – Debra, Sam, Emma

ACKNOWLEDGEMENTS

William and I thank a variety of people for their candid input on the first many drafts of this novel, which took many years to create and refine. I believe I had to get to know William well before I could write about him. It also takes courage to hand over your precious novel to others and ask for feedback. I am truly thankful for all of the amazing inputs I received.